GN

I Go Quiet

David Ouimet

CANONGATE

First published in Great Britain in 2019 by Canongate Books Ltd,
14 High Street, Edinburgh EH1 1TE

canongate.co.uk

1

British Library Cataloguing-in-Publication Data
A catalogue record for this book is available on
request from the British Library

ISBN 978 1 78689 740 4

Printed and bound in China by C&C (Offset)

MIX
Paper from responsible sources
FSC® C008047
www.fsc.org

For Gabrielle

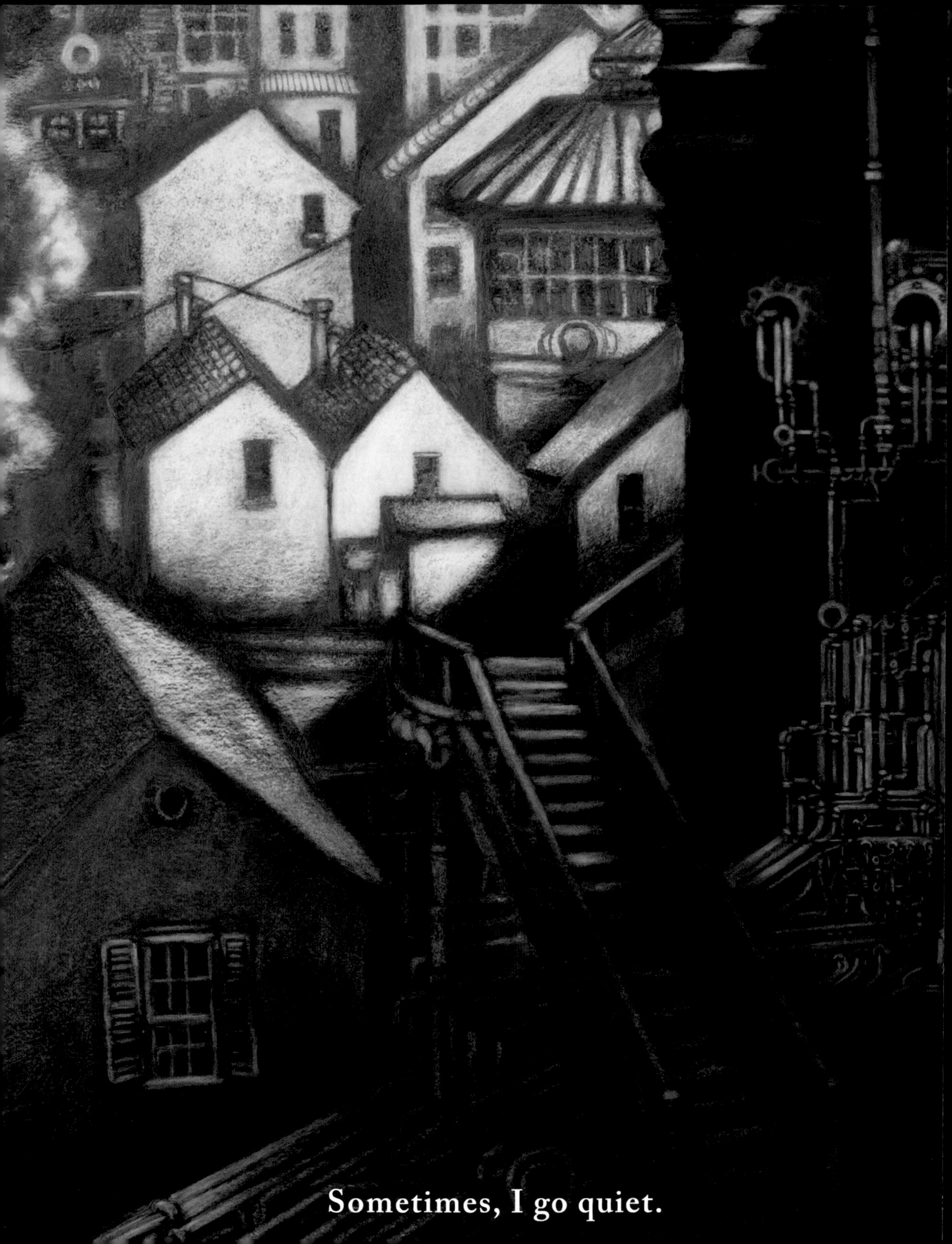

Sometimes, I go quiet.

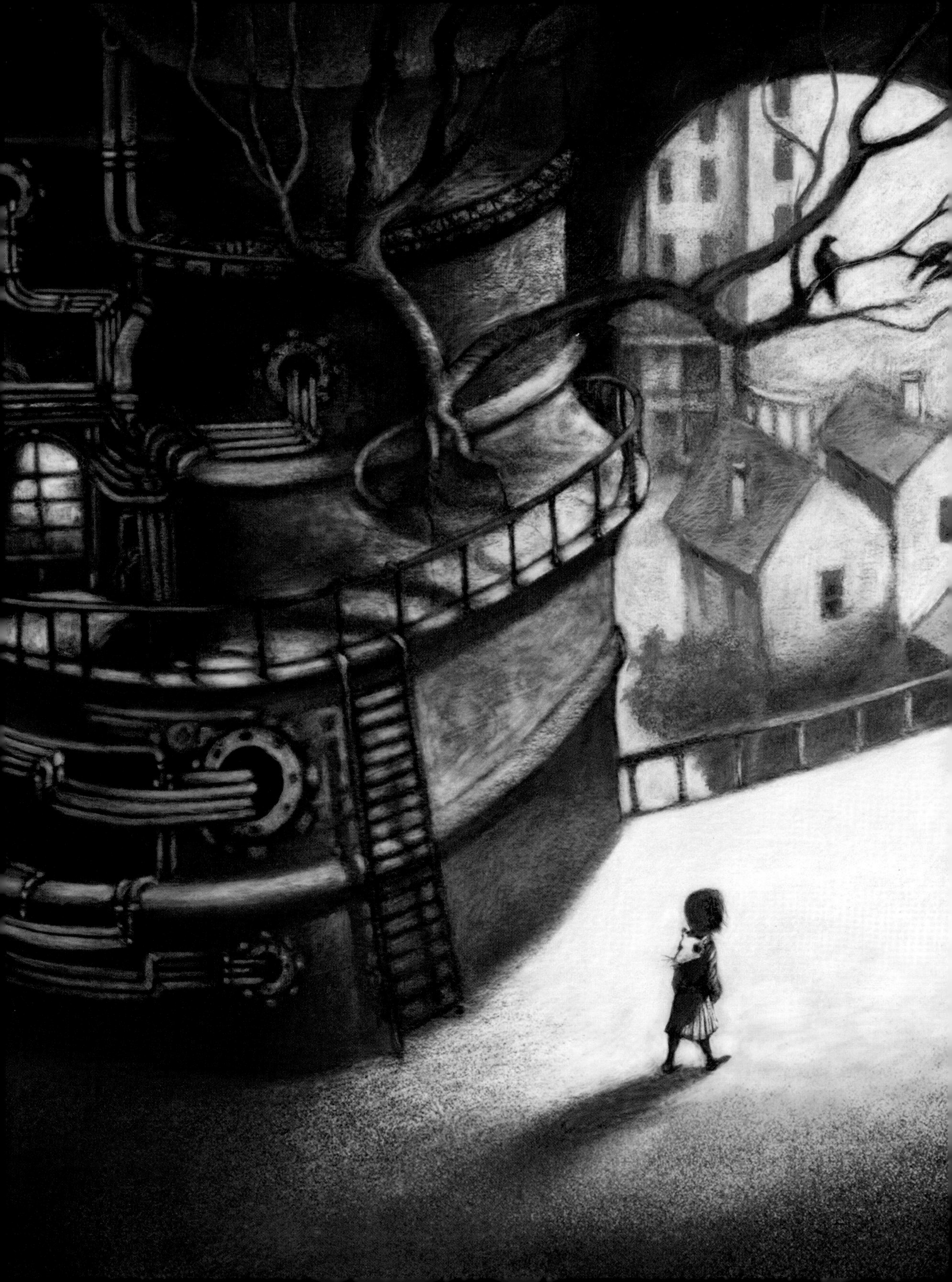

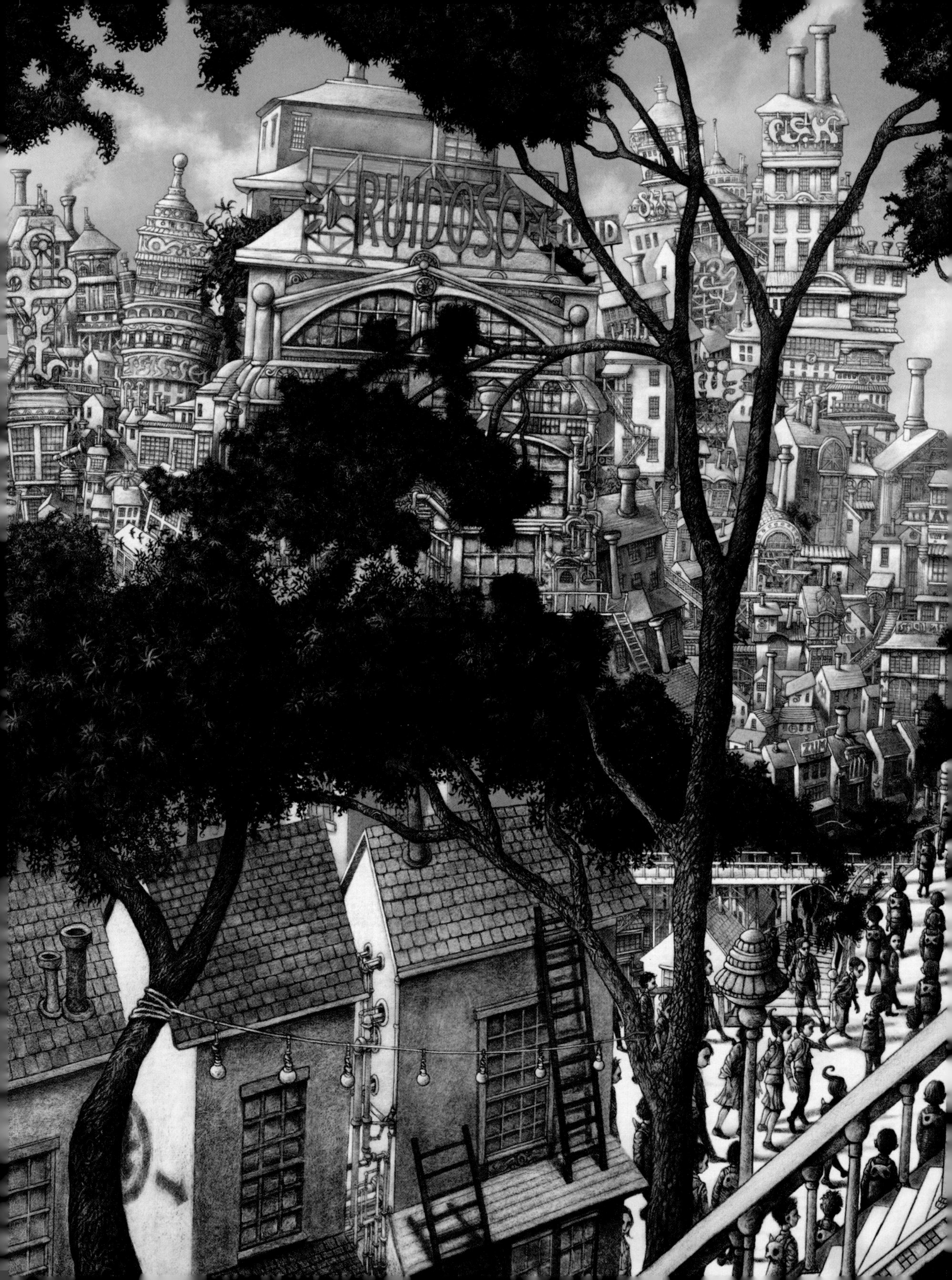
RUIDOSO

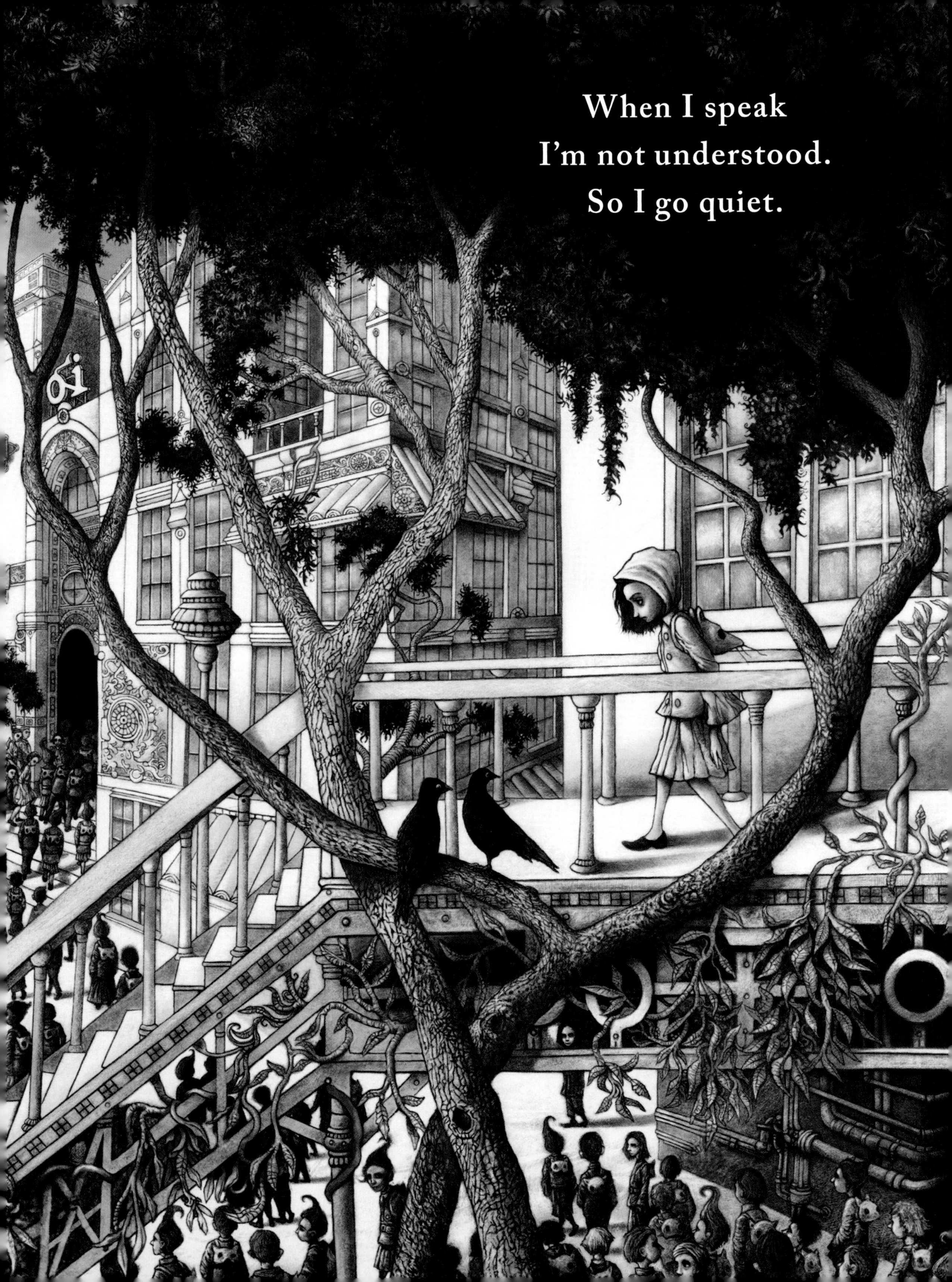

When I speak
I'm not understood.
So I go quiet.

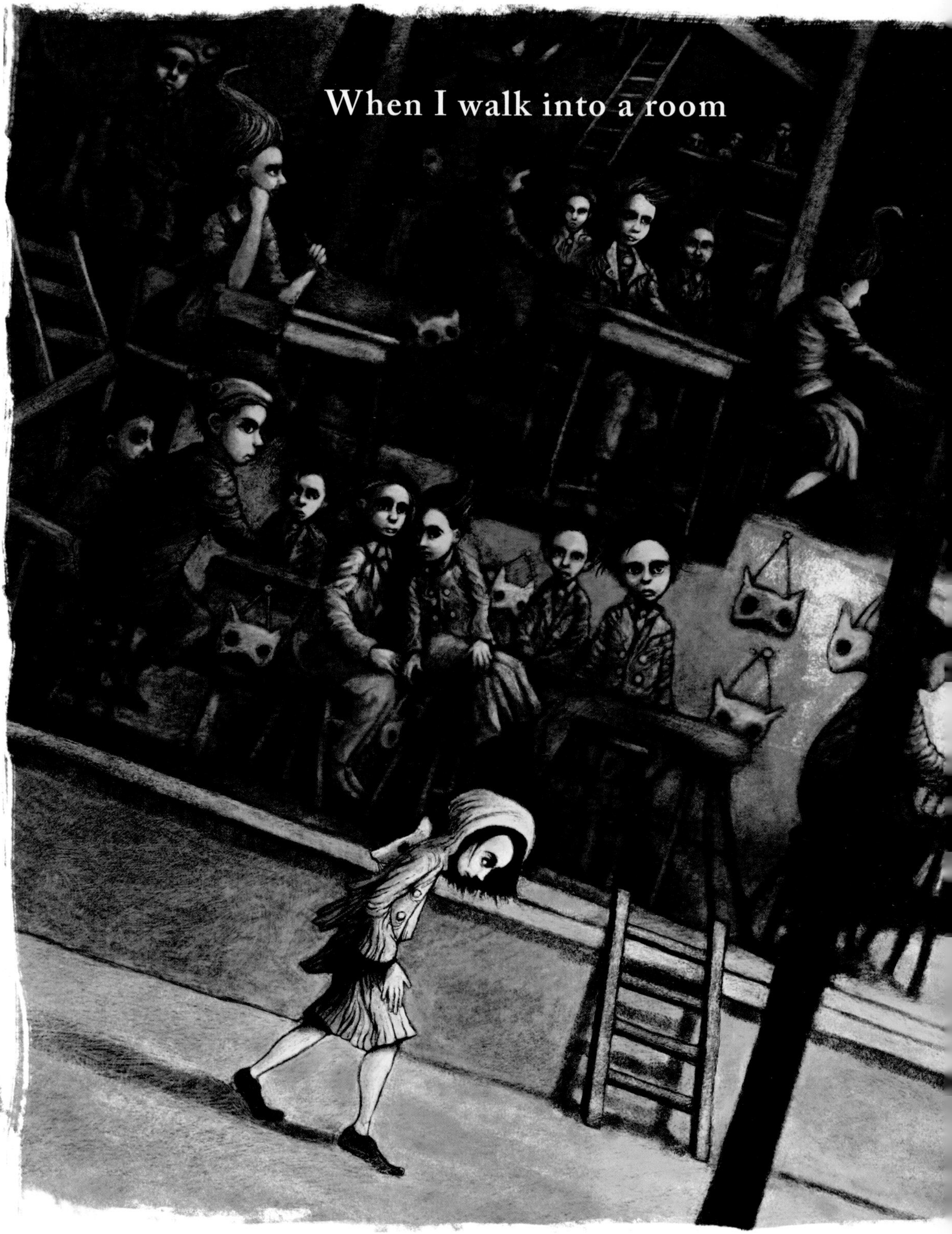

When I walk into a room

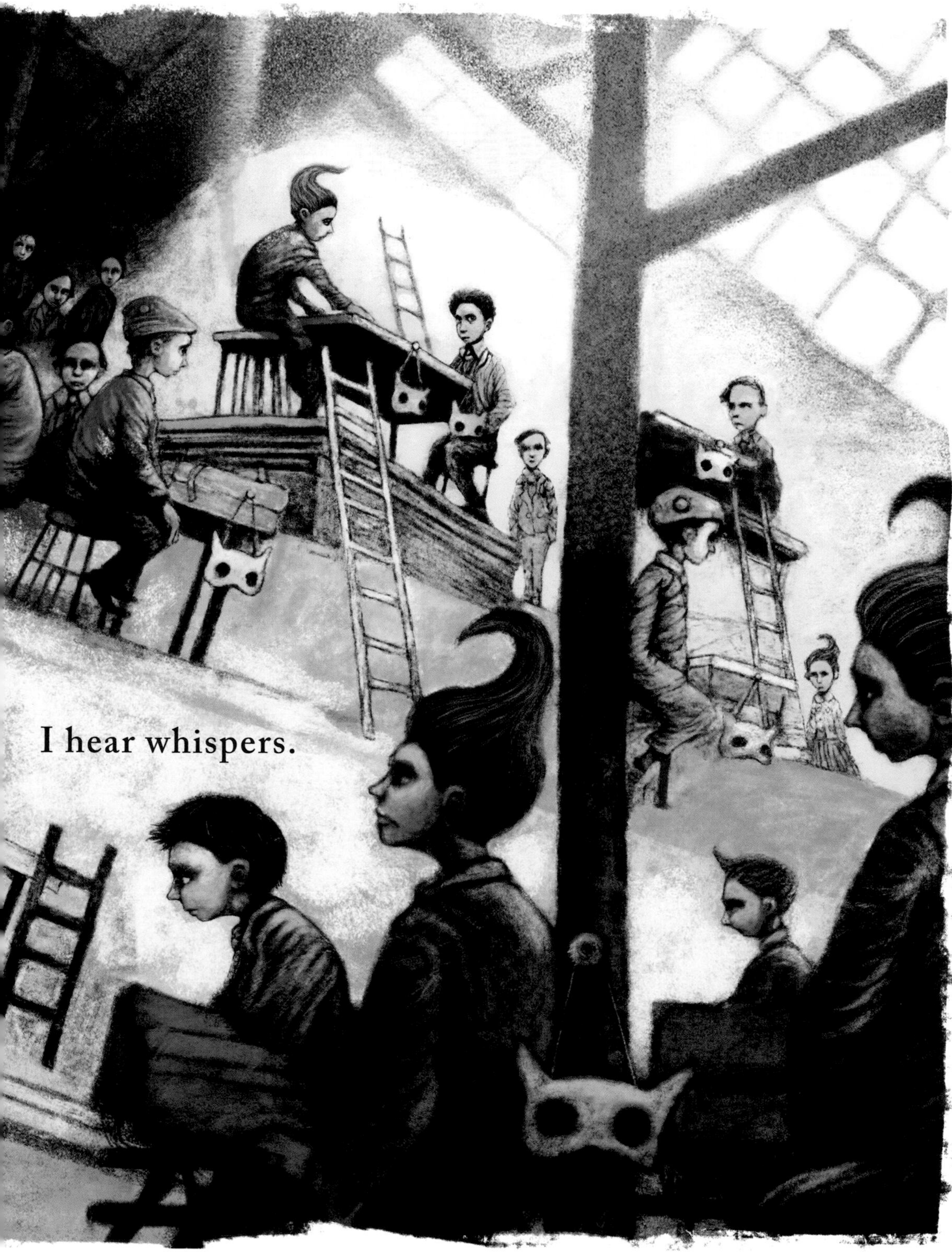

I hear whispers.

I don't know how I am supposed to be.

I am timid. I am small.
How should I sound?
How should I look?
When it's my turn
to speak,
I go

quiet.

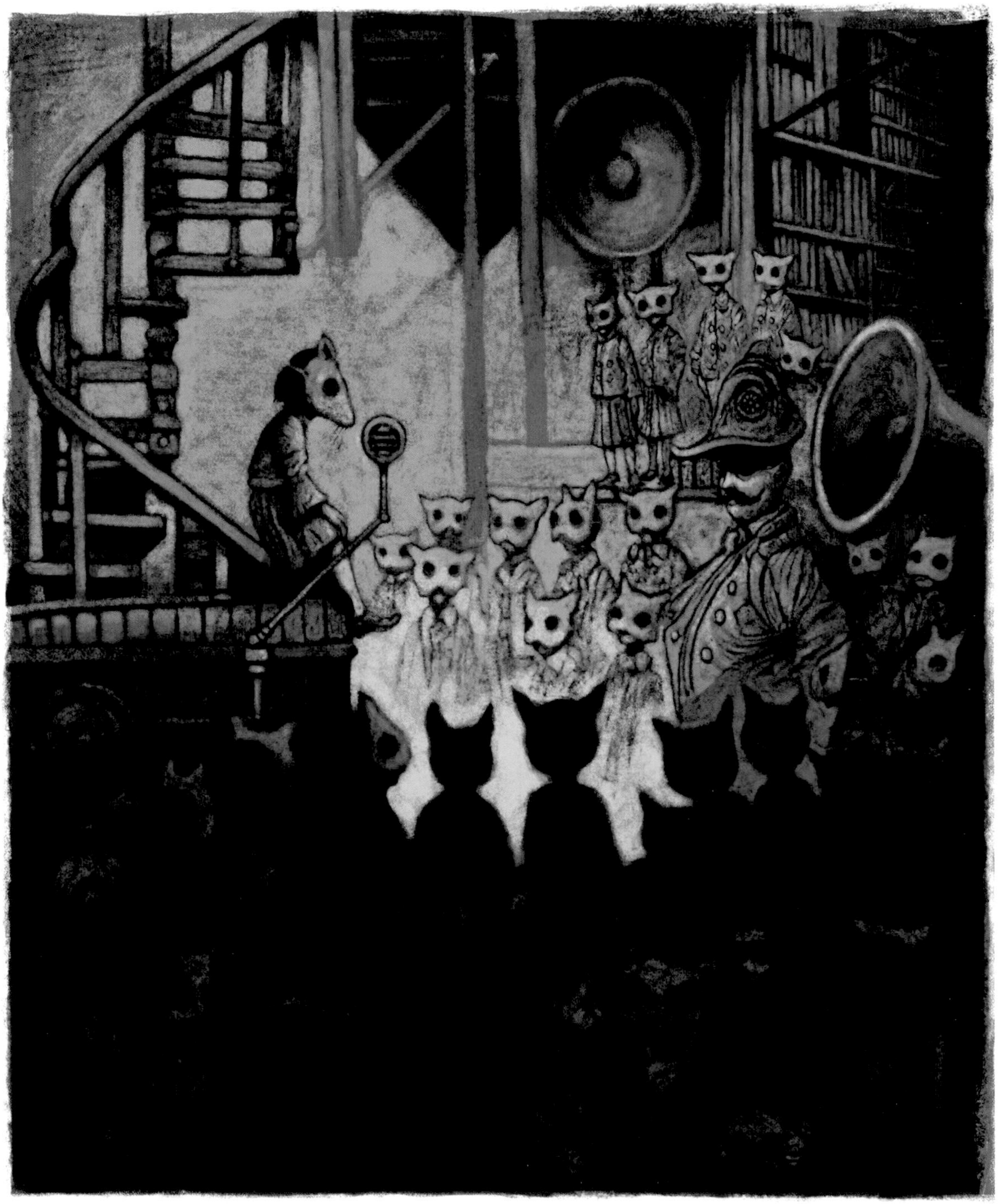

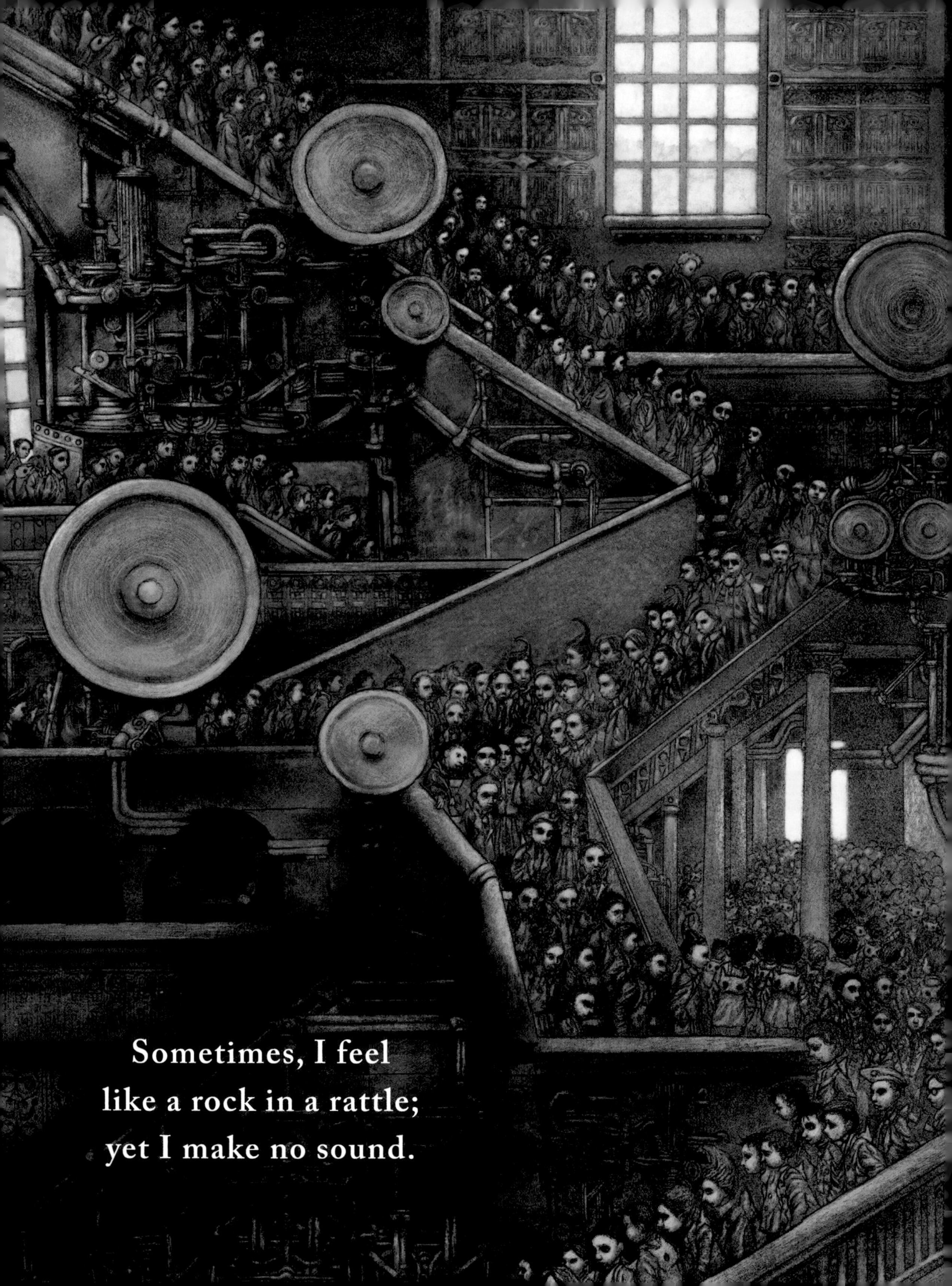

Sometimes, I feel
like a rock in a rattle;
yet I make no sound.

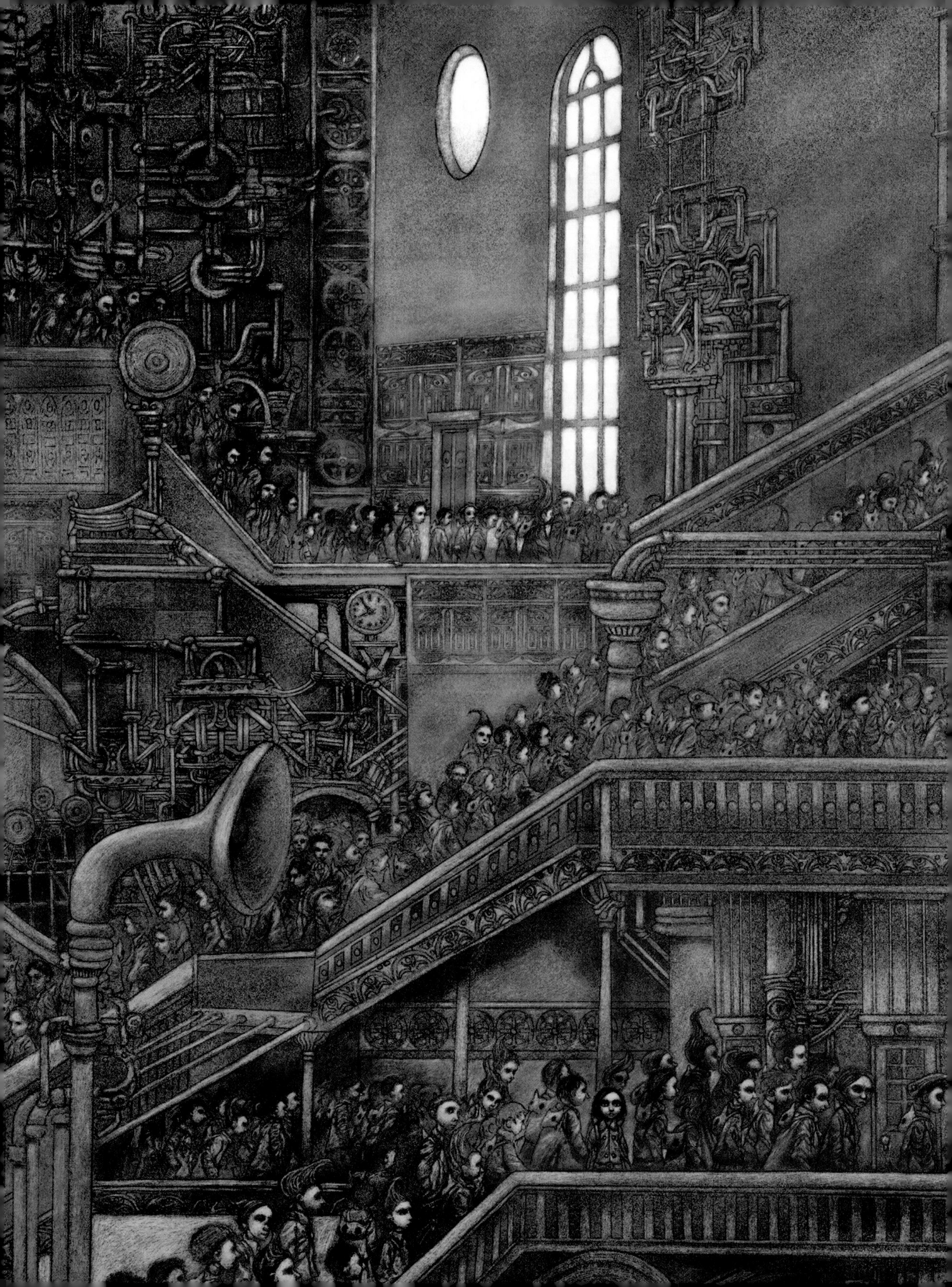

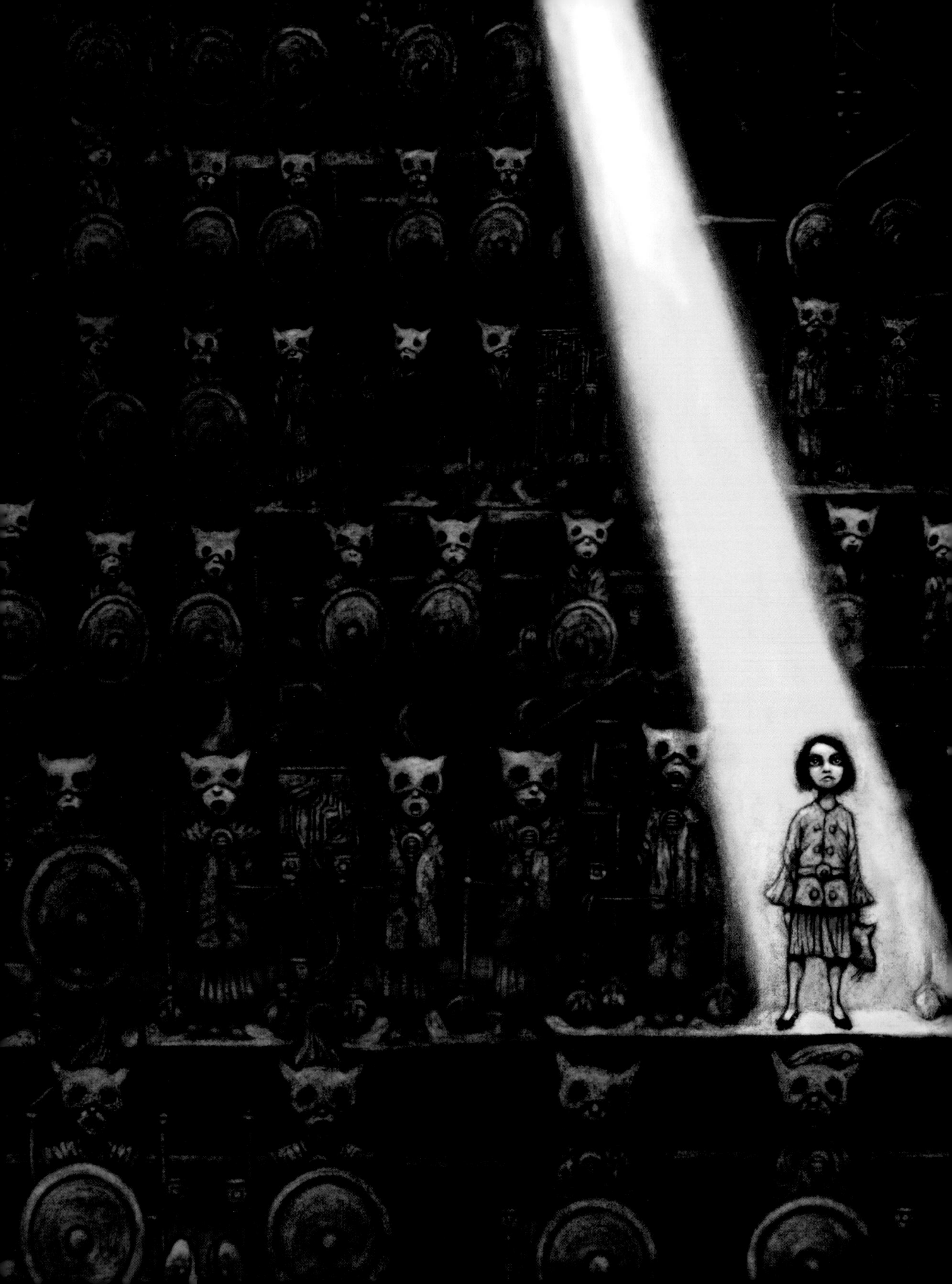

I am different.
I am the note
that's not in tune.
I go mousy. I go grey.

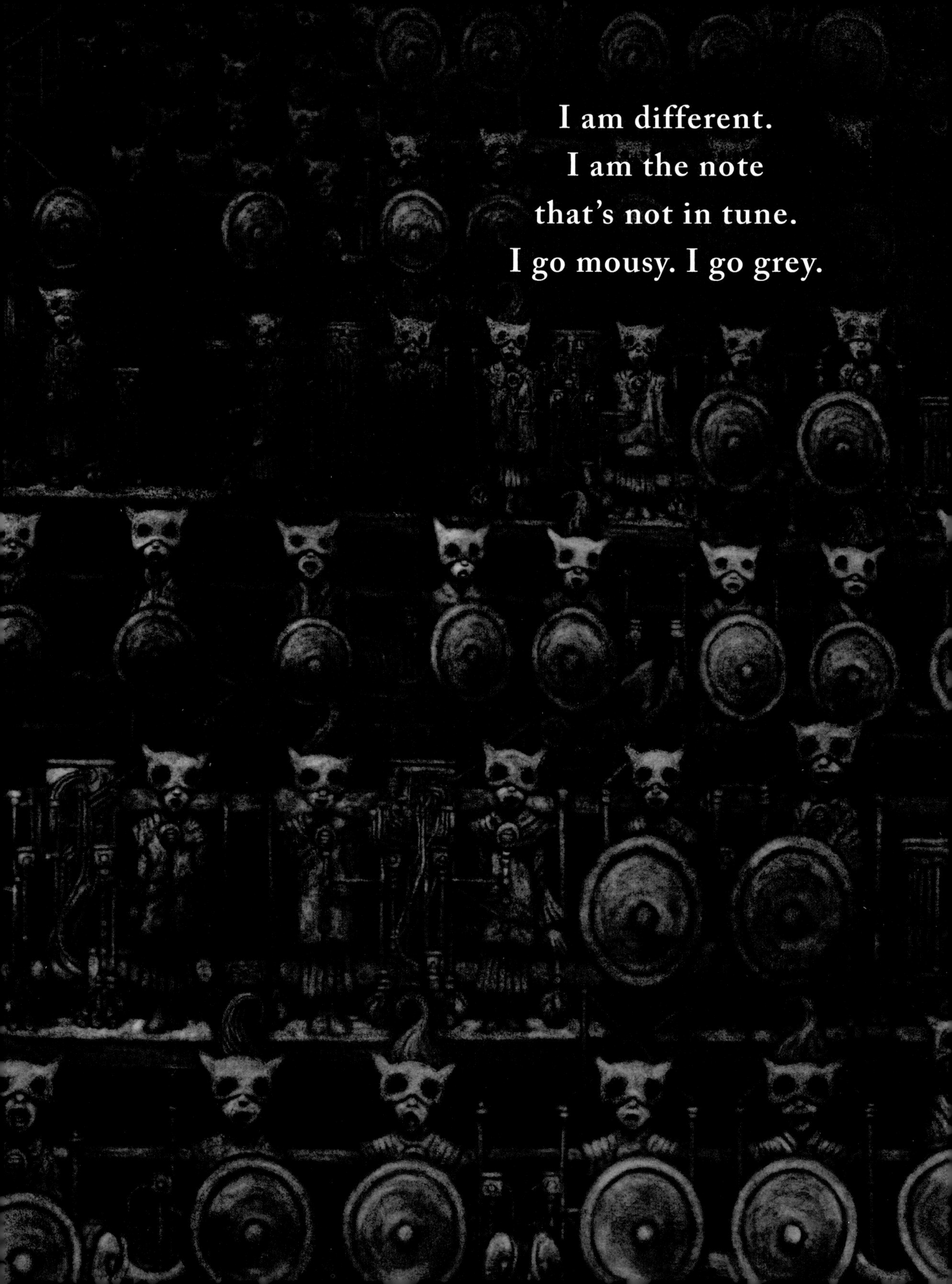

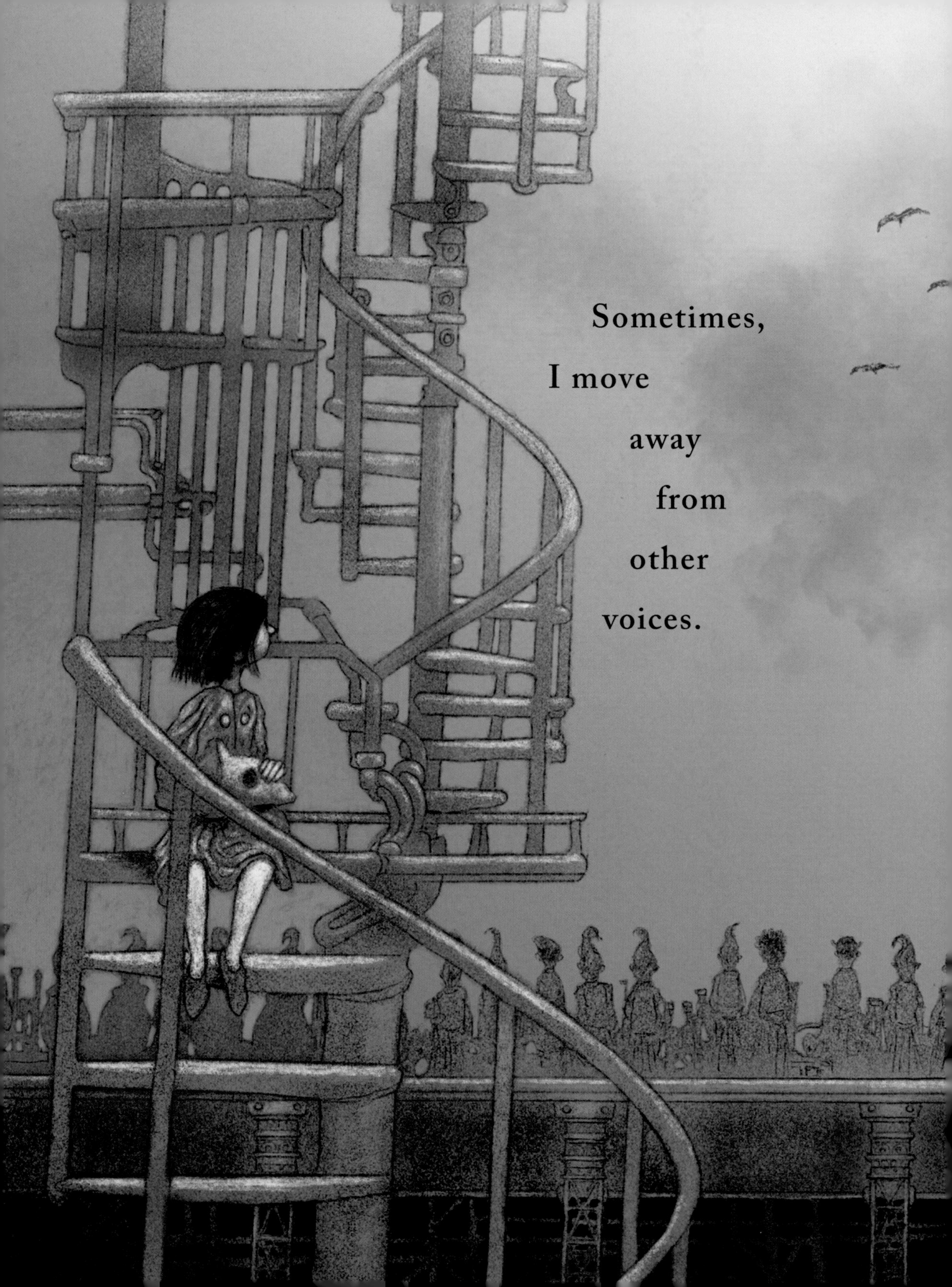

Sometimes,
I move
away
from
other
voices.

I sing silence as loud as I can.

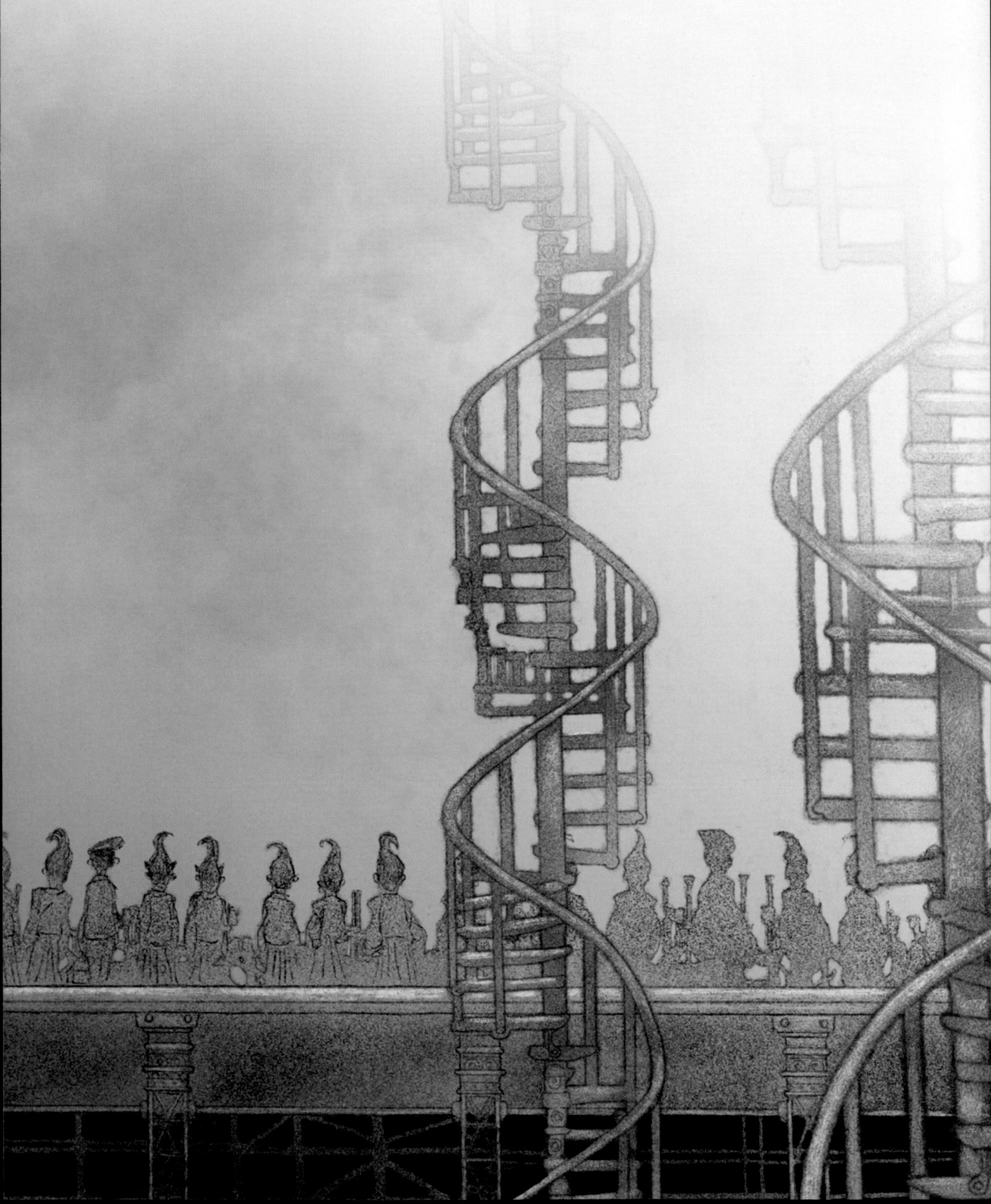

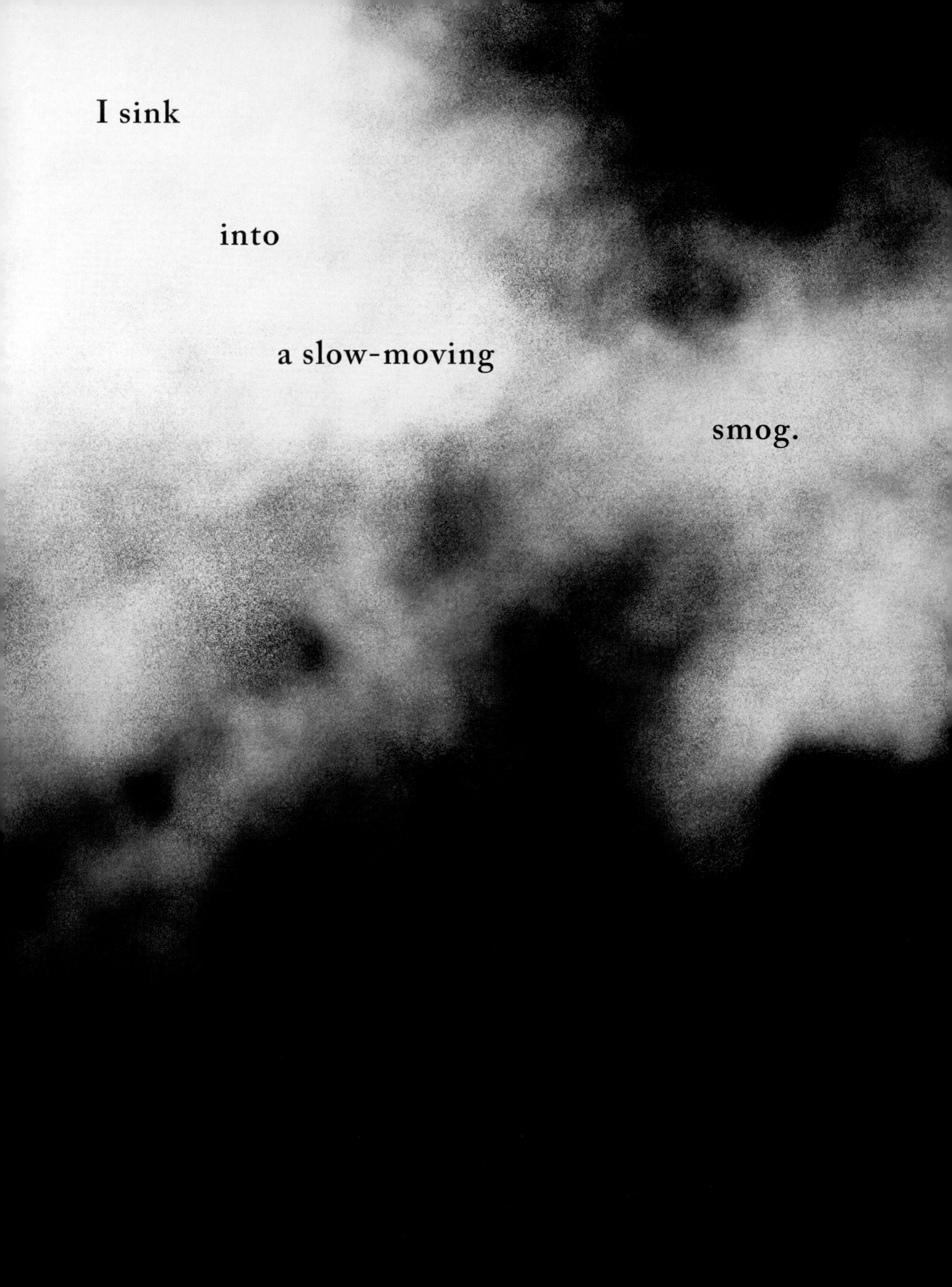

I sink

into

a slow-moving

smog.

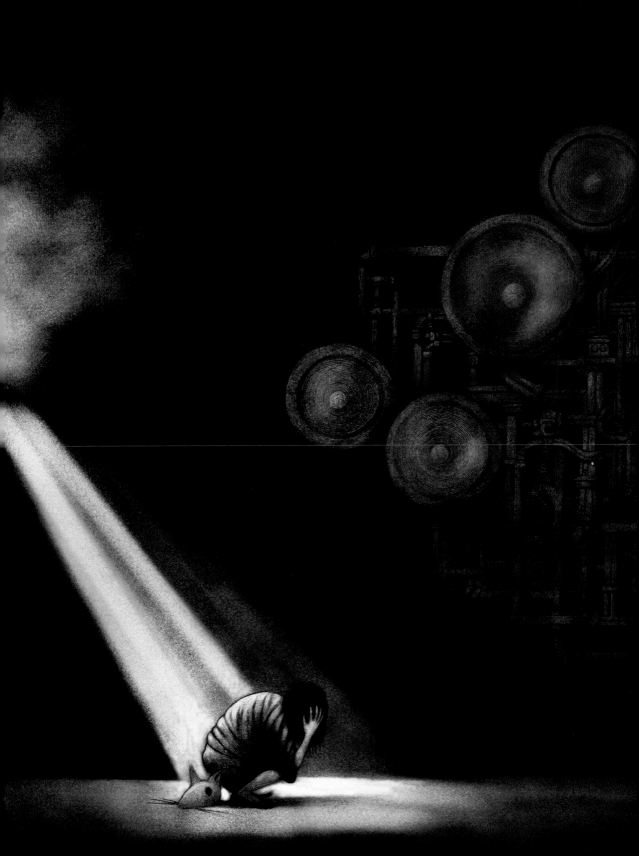

I don't always listen.

My thoughts wander to other things.

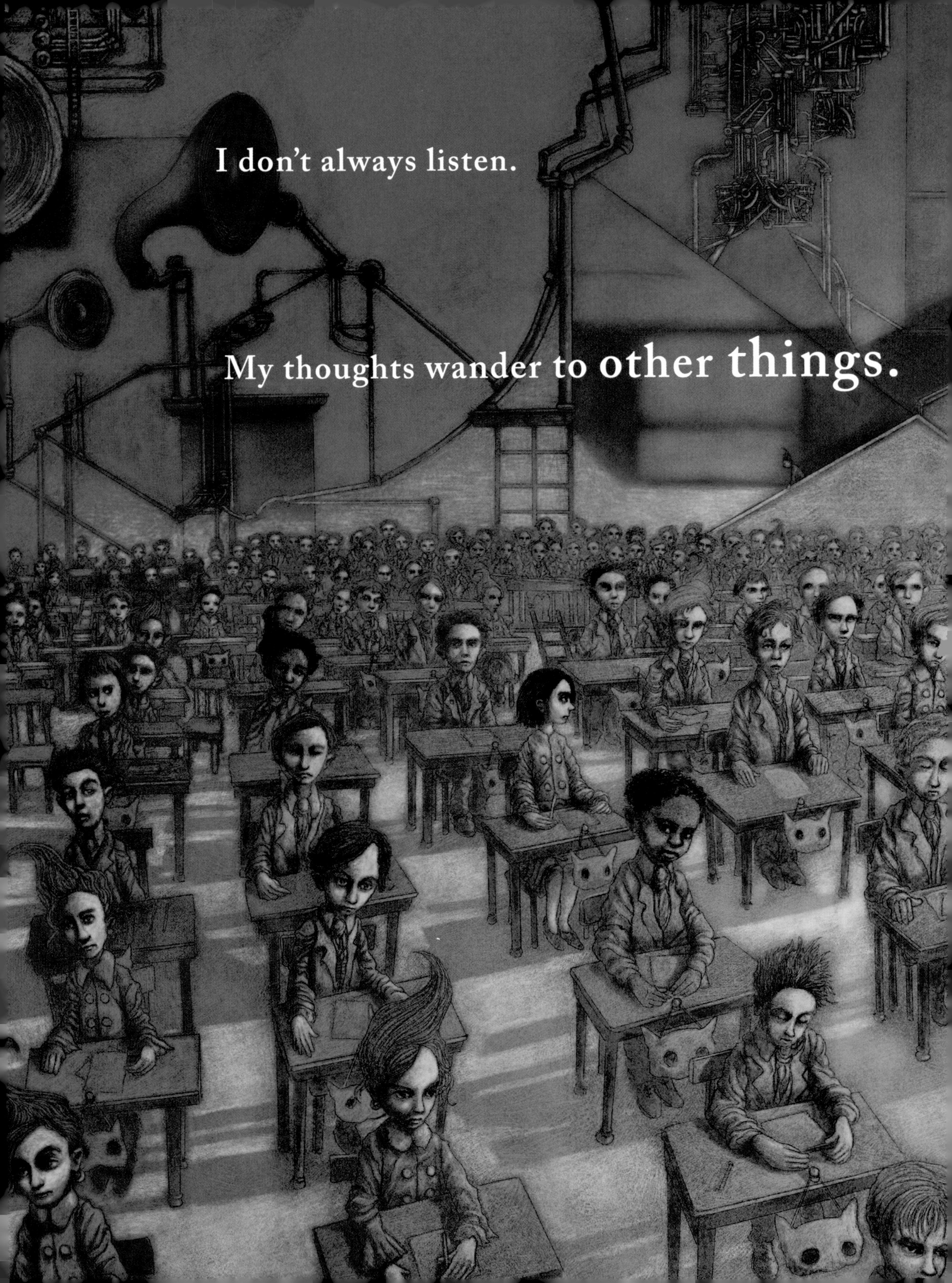

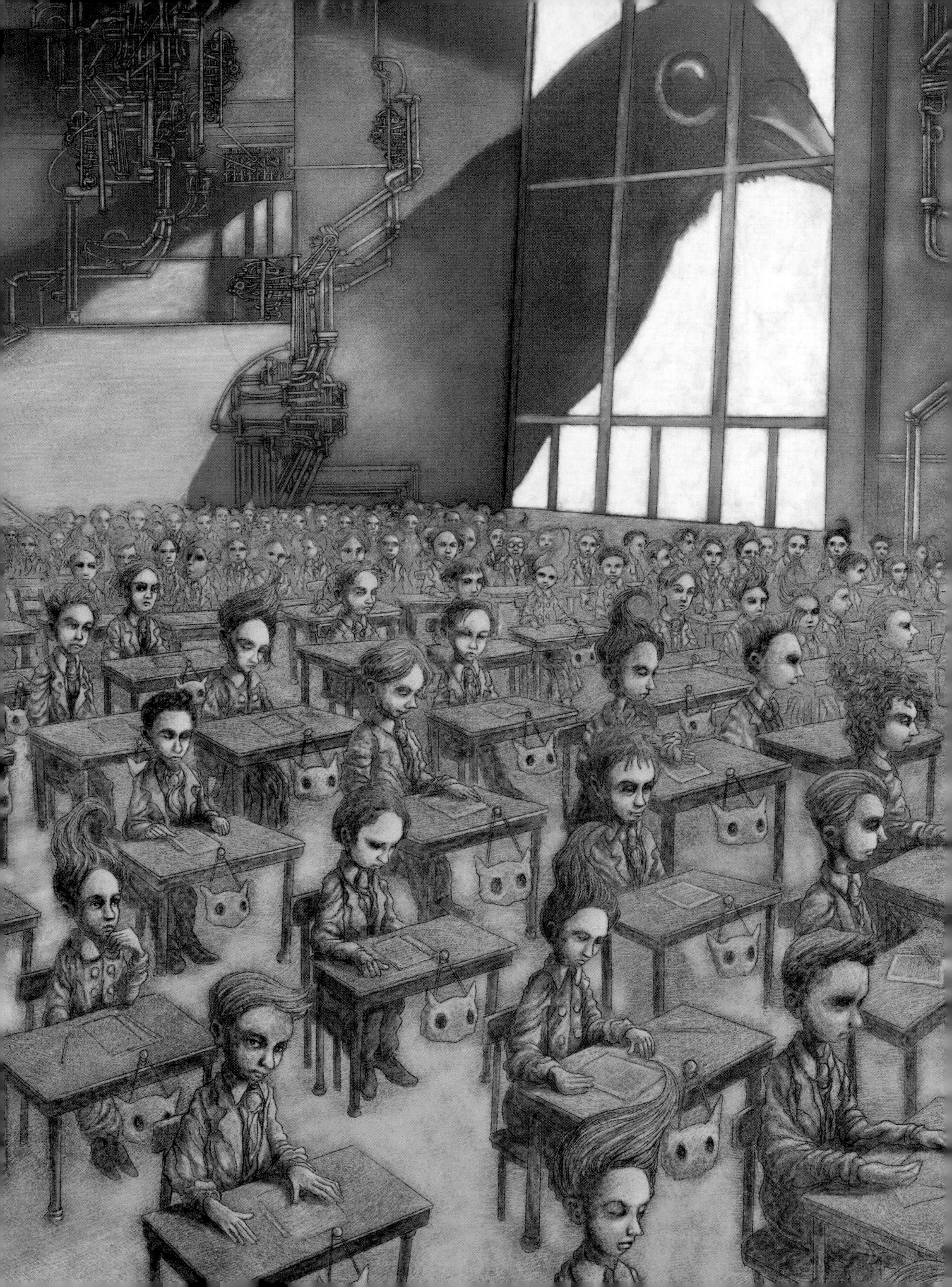

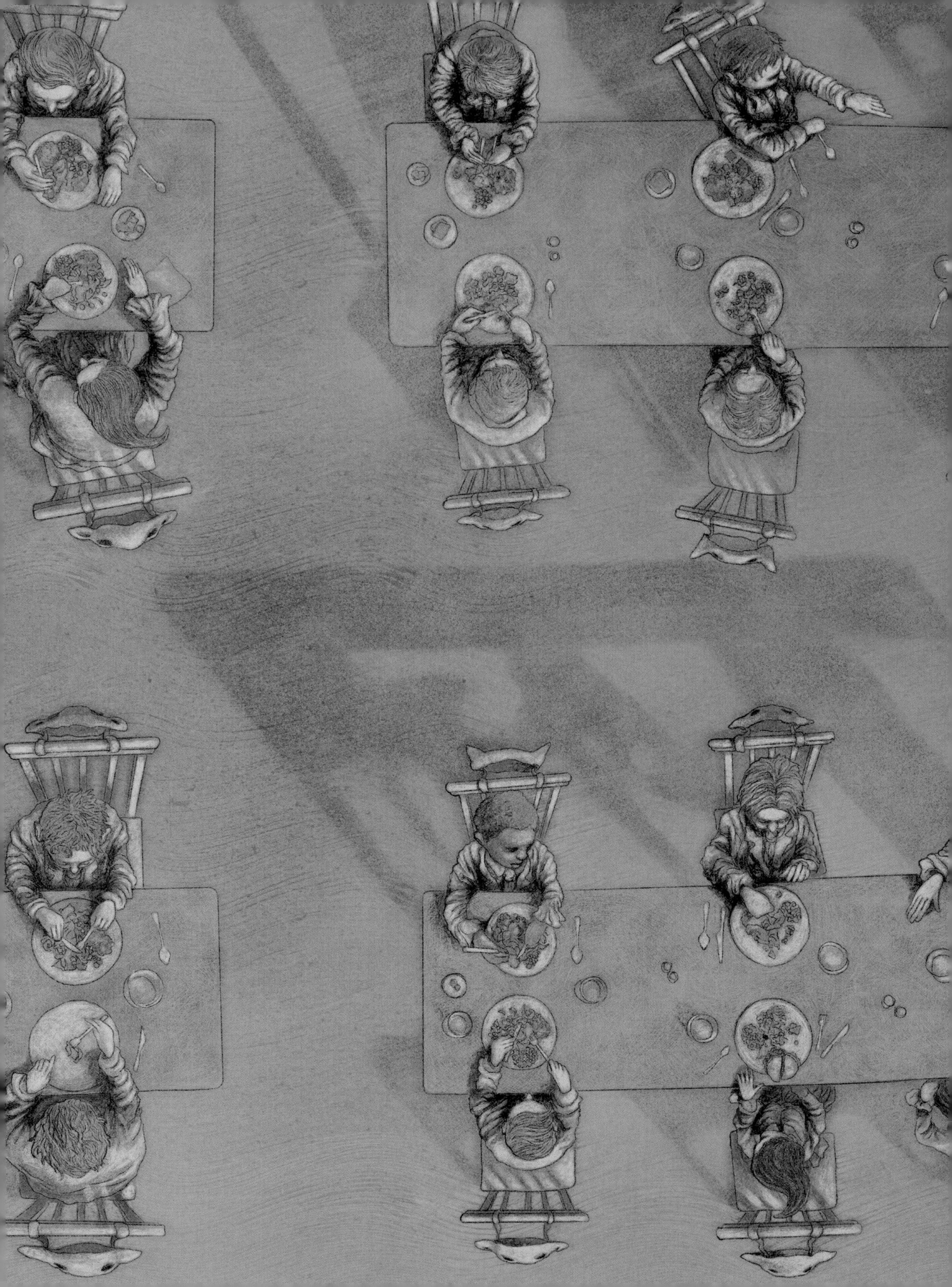

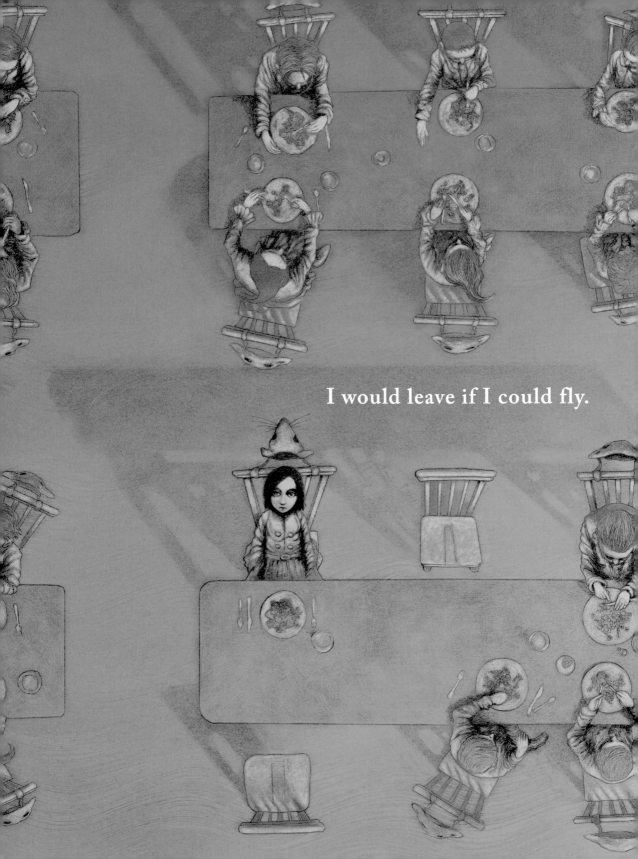

I would leave if I could fly.

From time to time I imagine

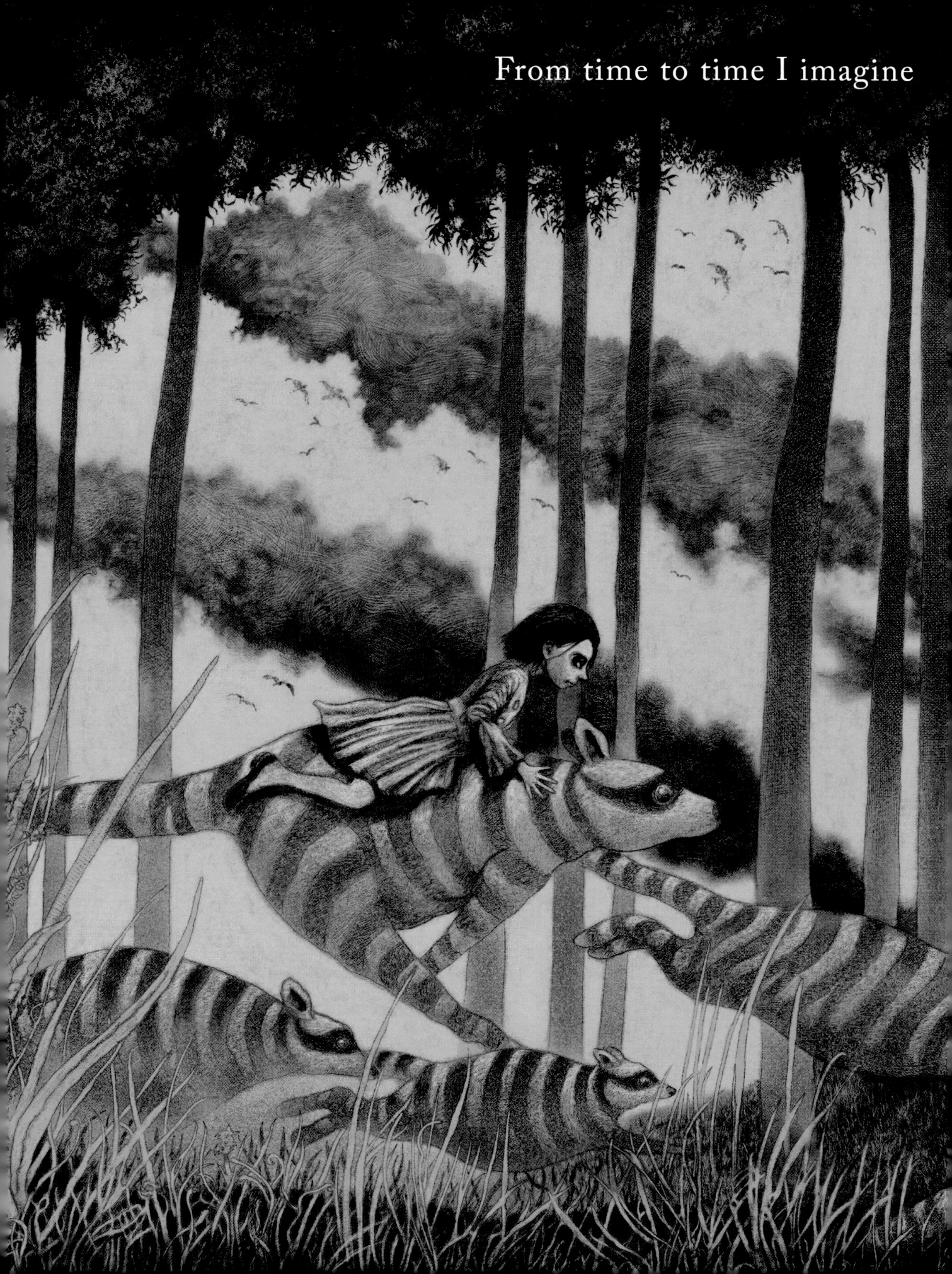

where I'd like to be.

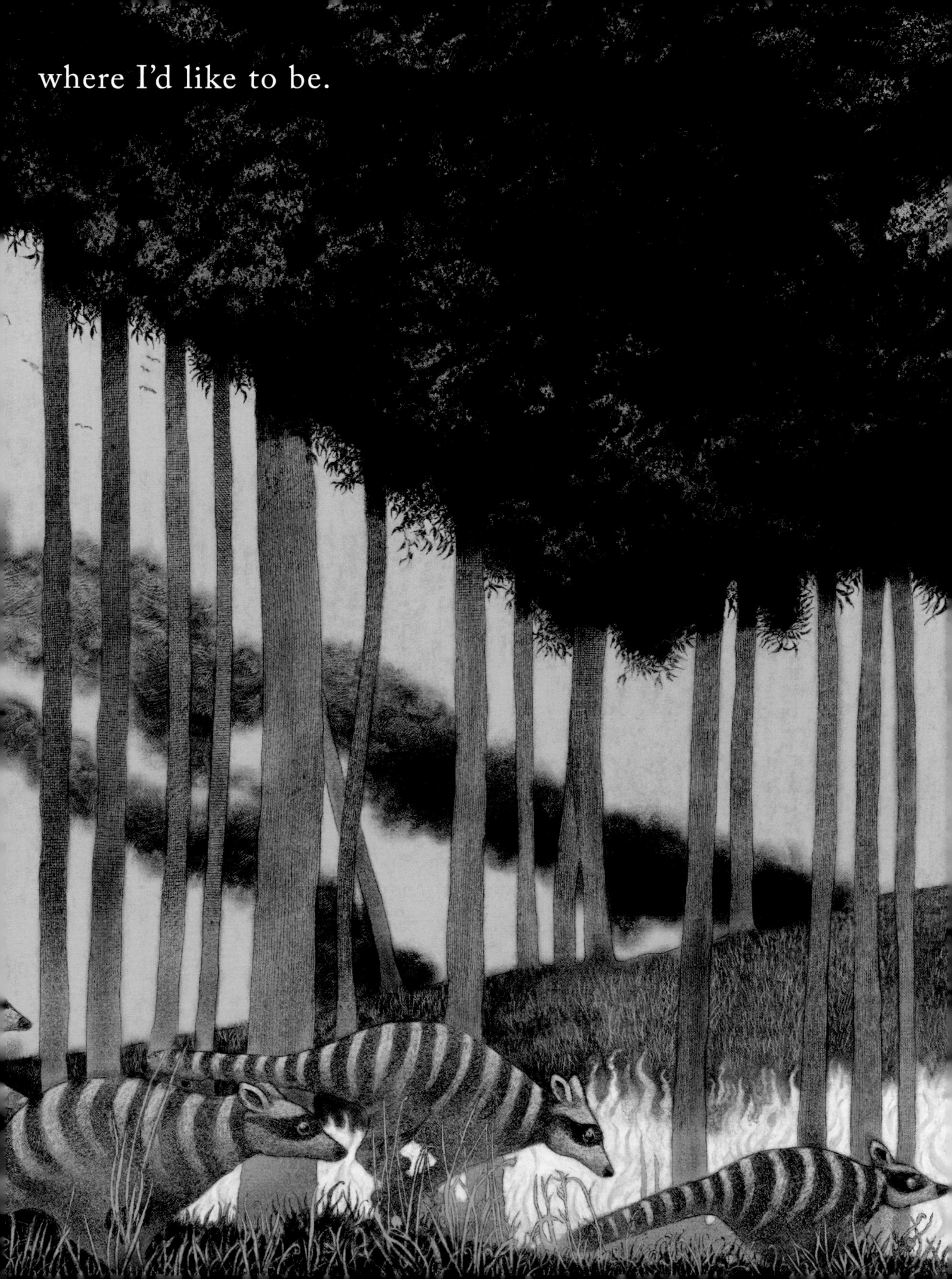

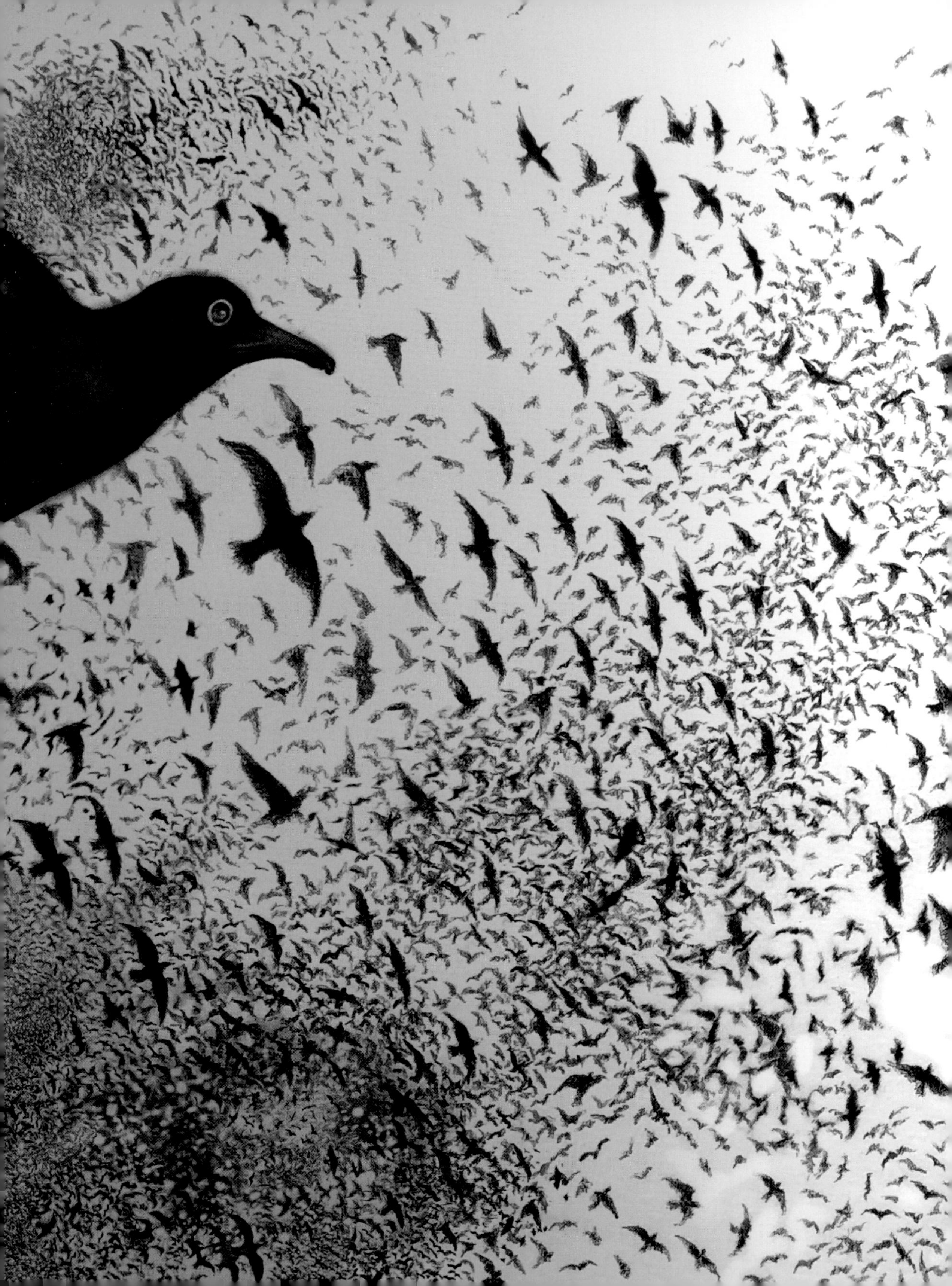

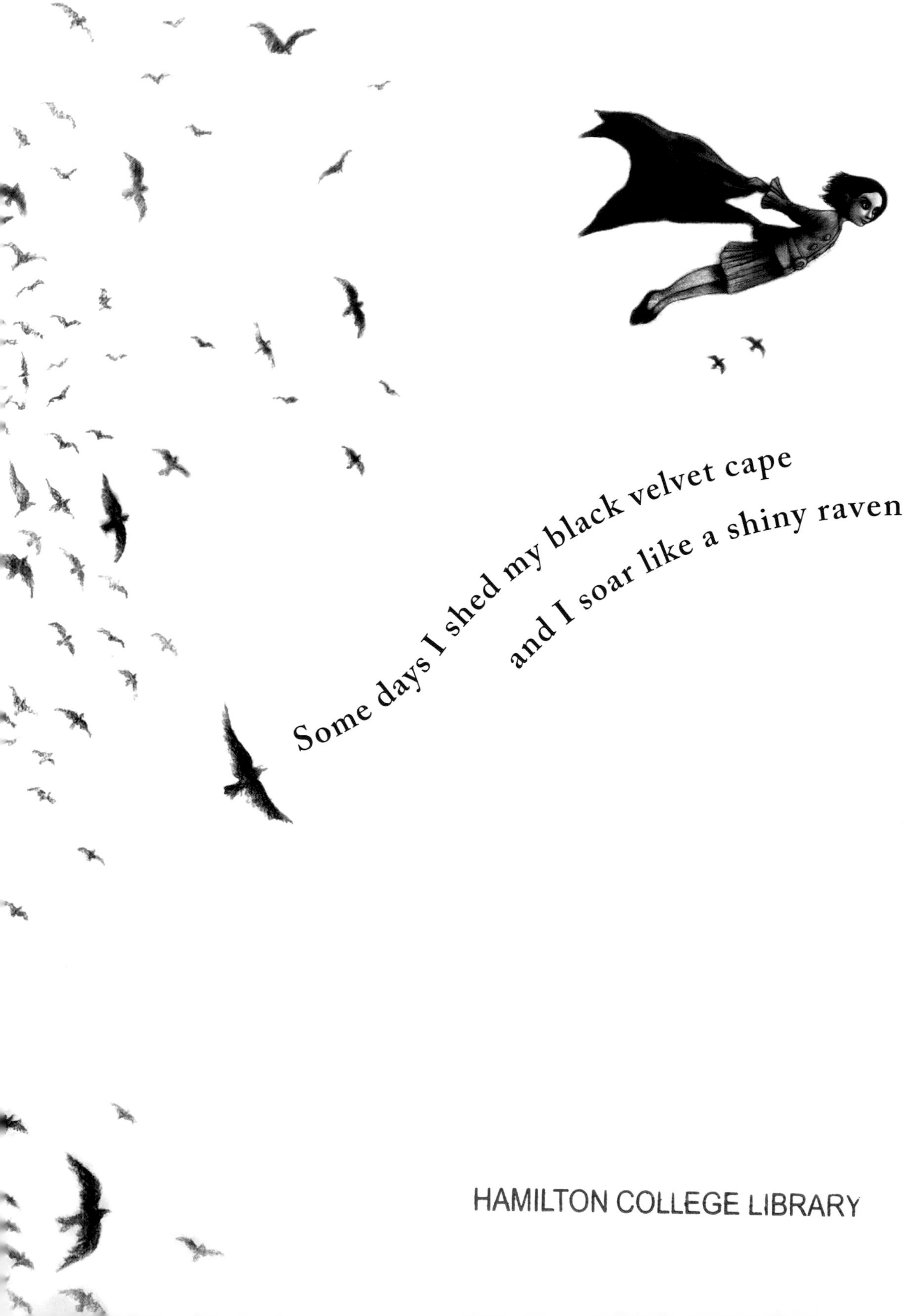

Some days I shed my black velvet cape
and I soar like a shiny raven.

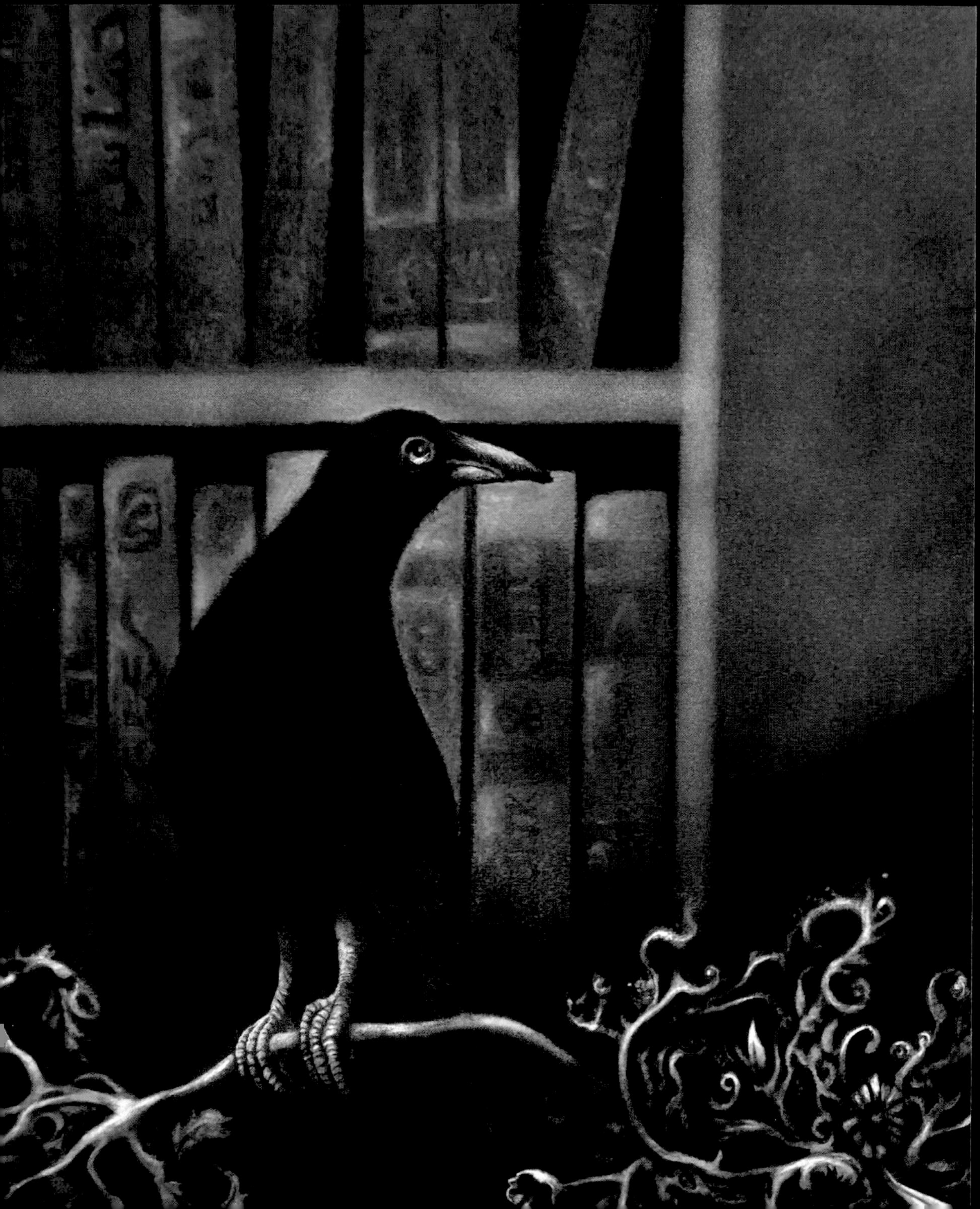

Sometimes, when I go quiet I read.

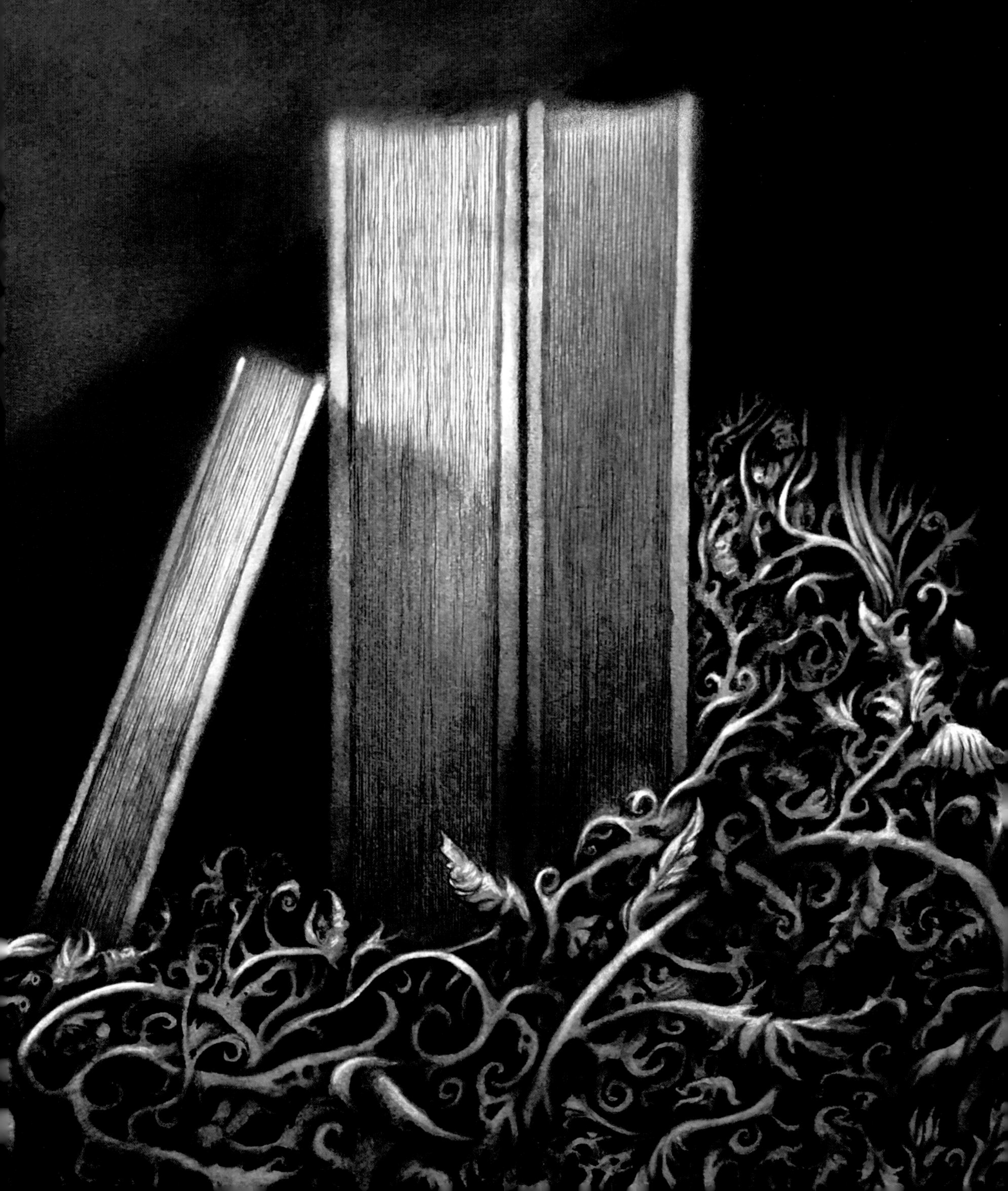

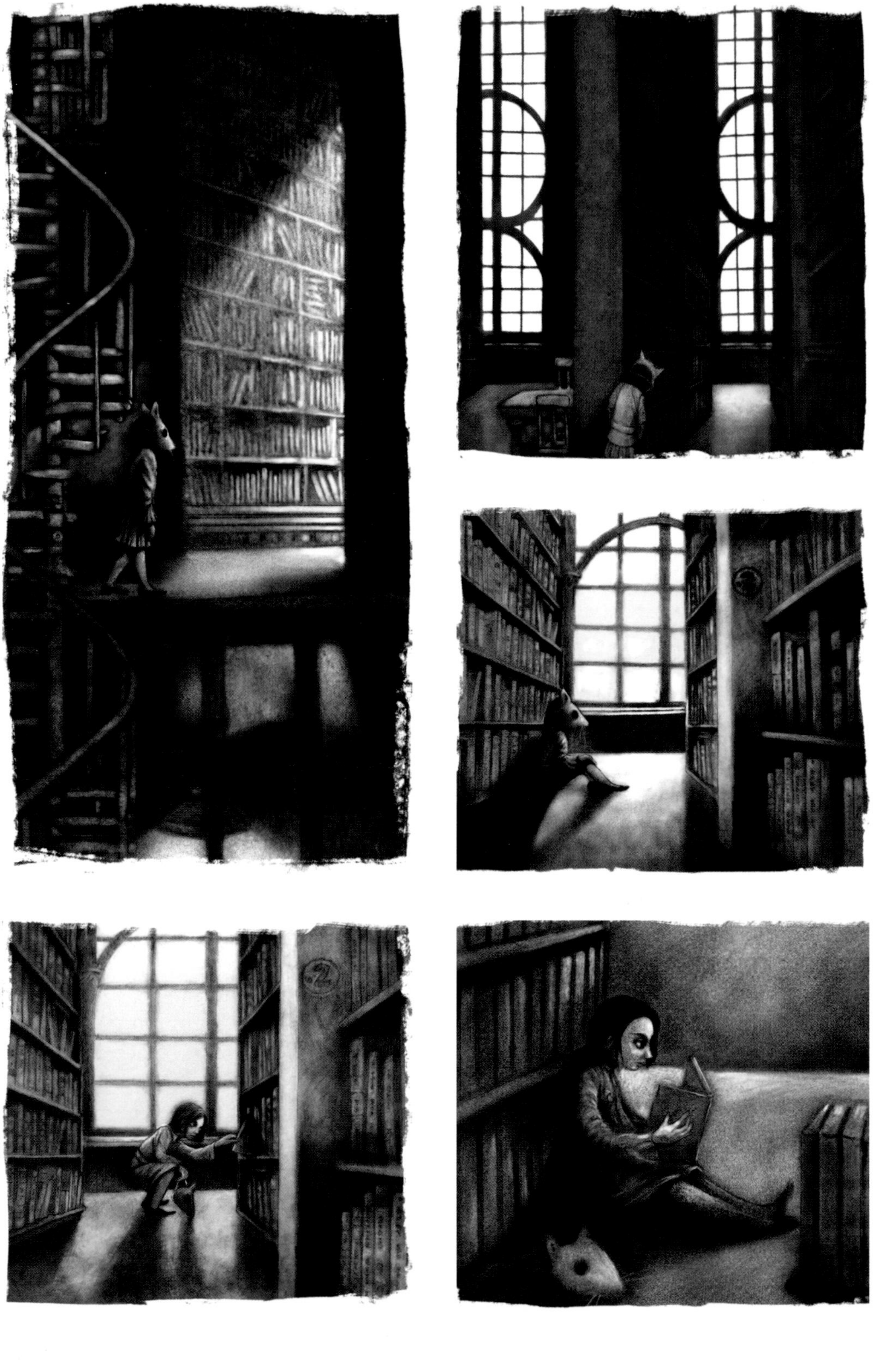

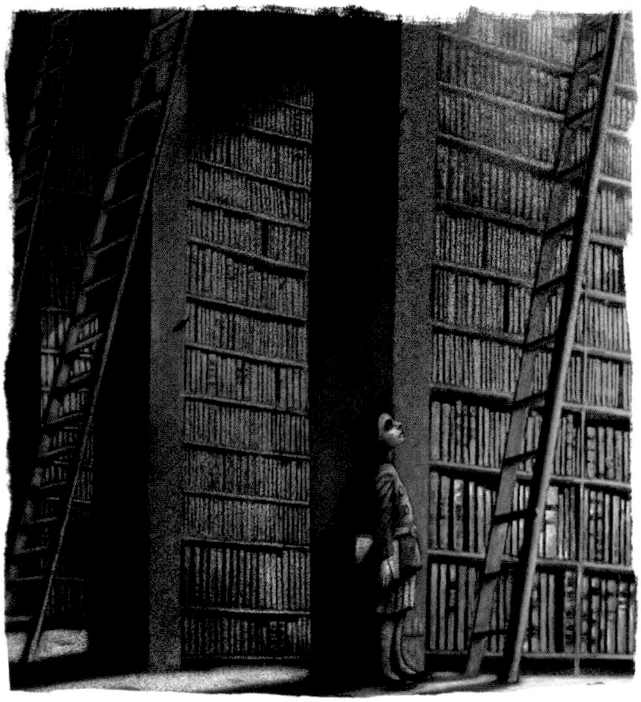 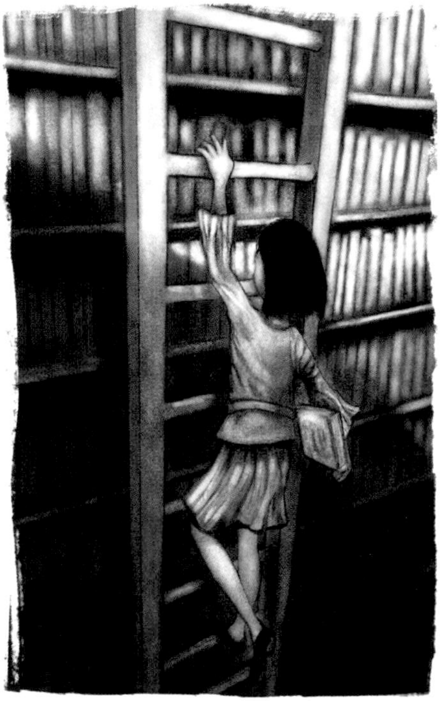

When I read, I know there are languages that I will speak.

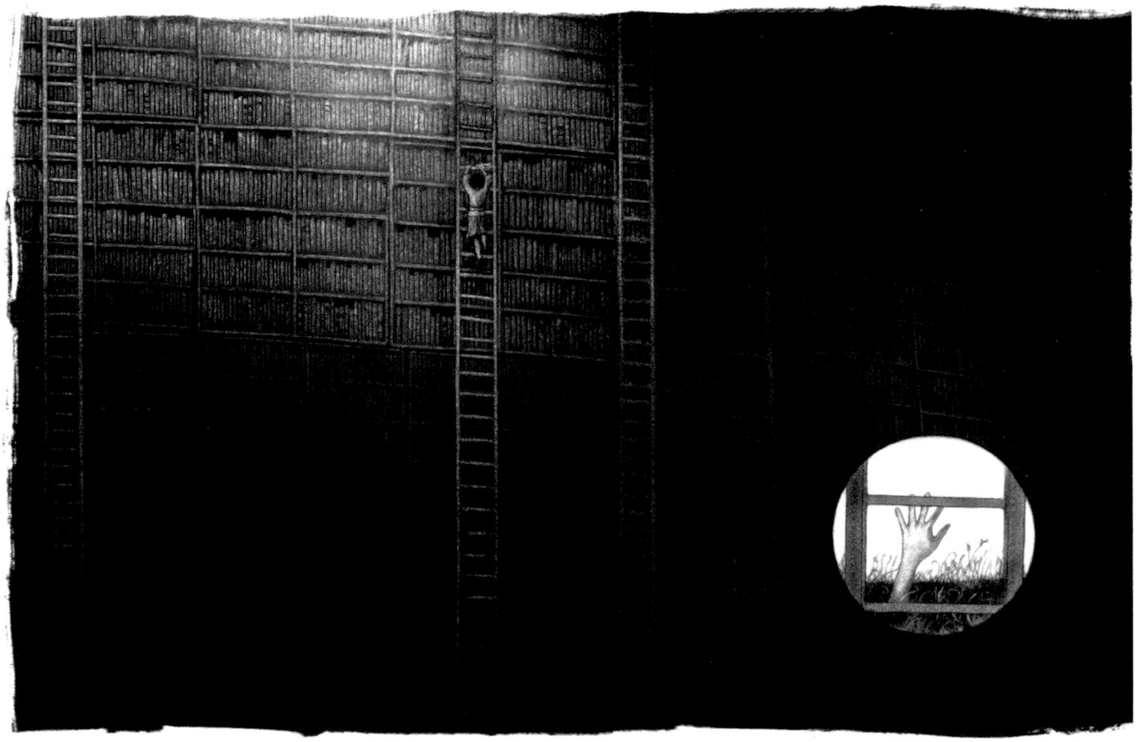

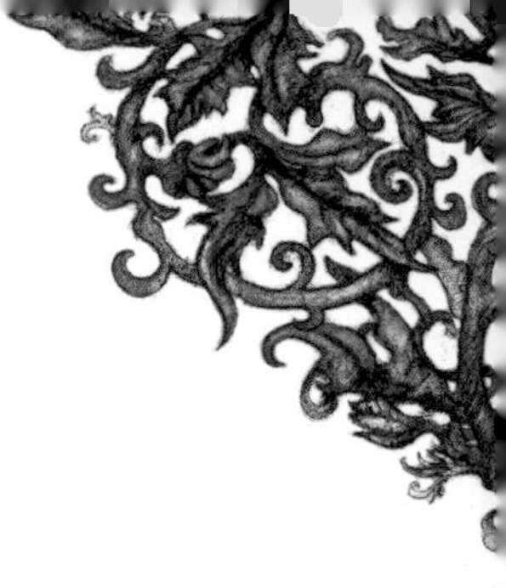

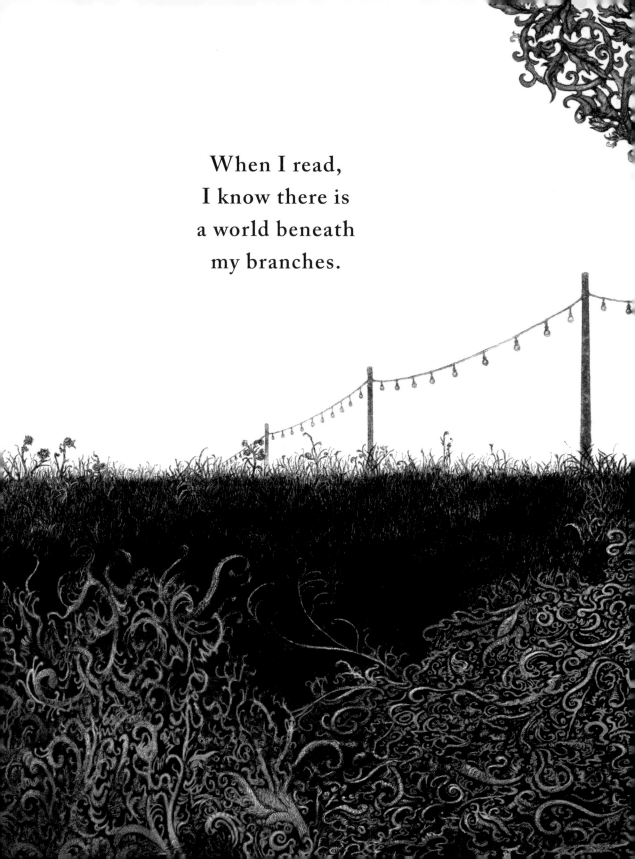

When I read,
I know there is
a world beneath
my branches.

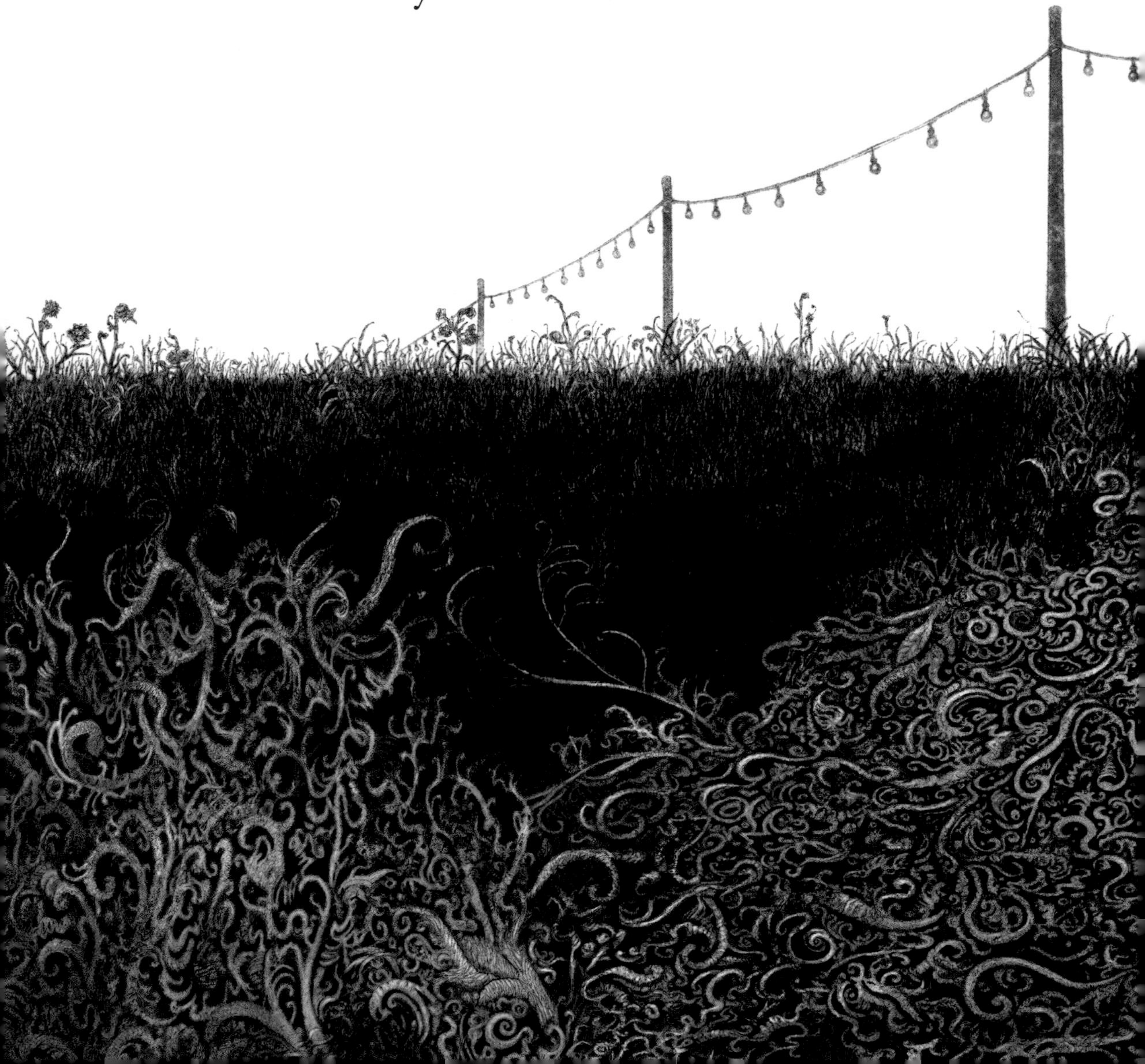

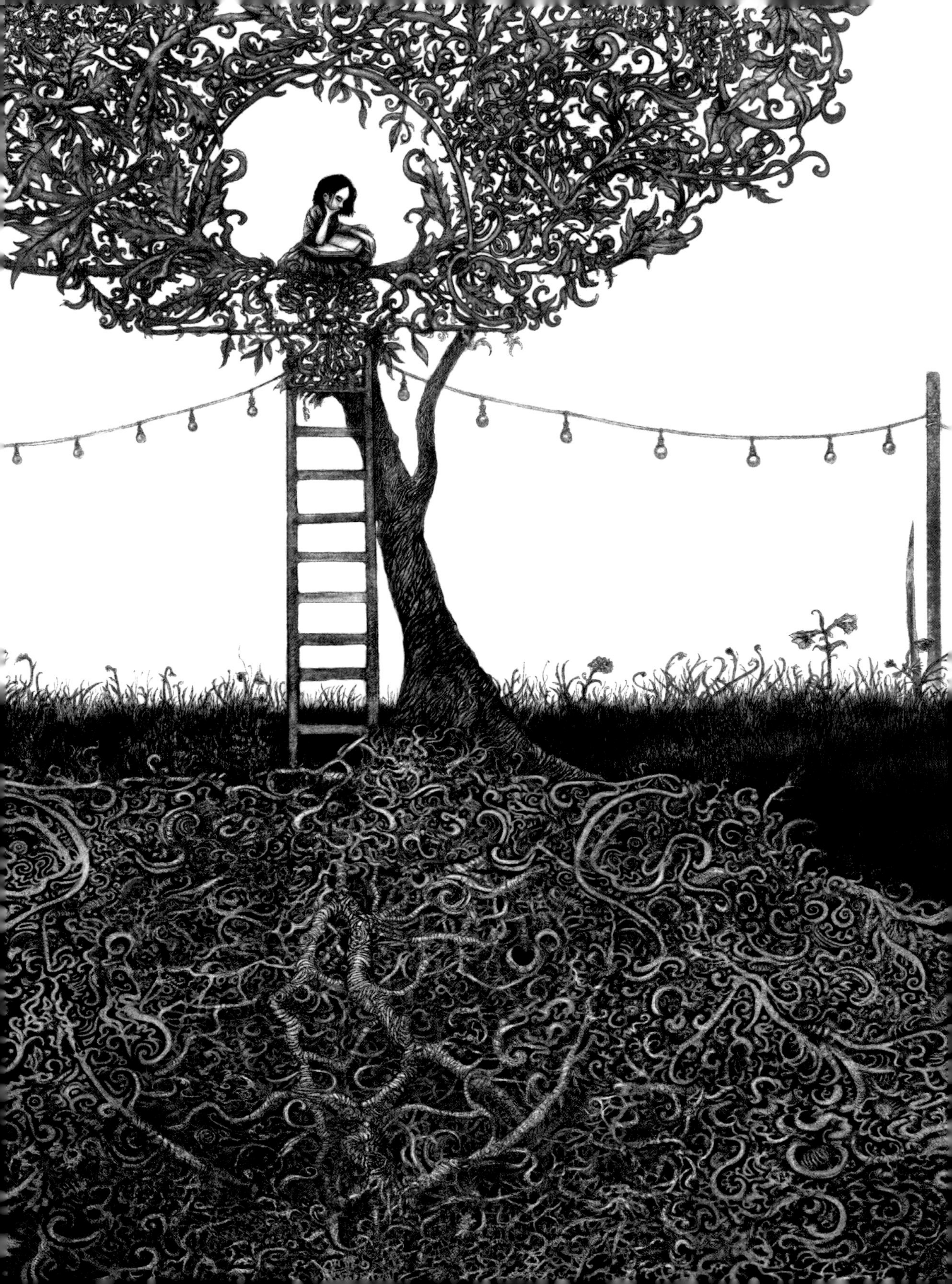

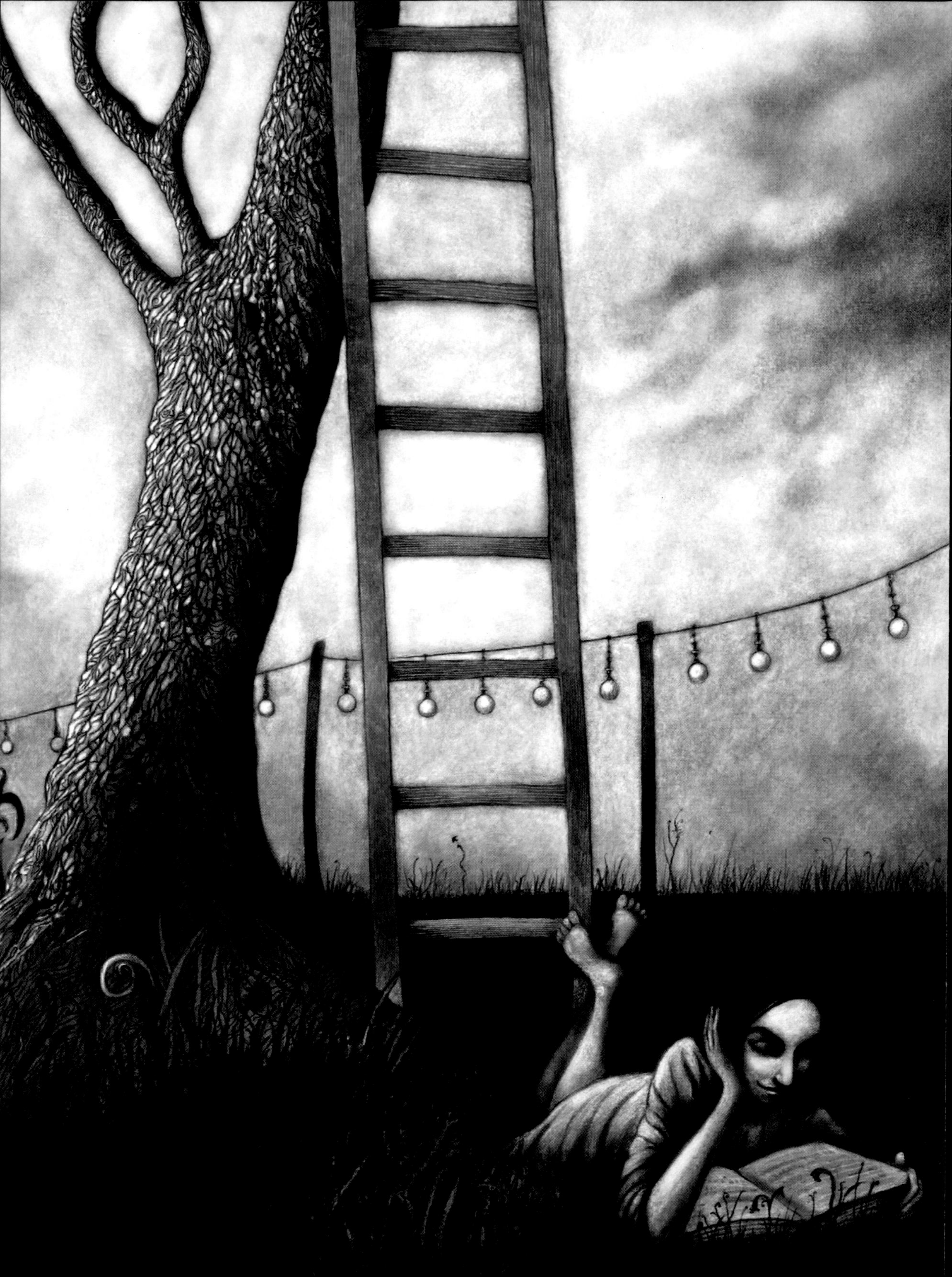

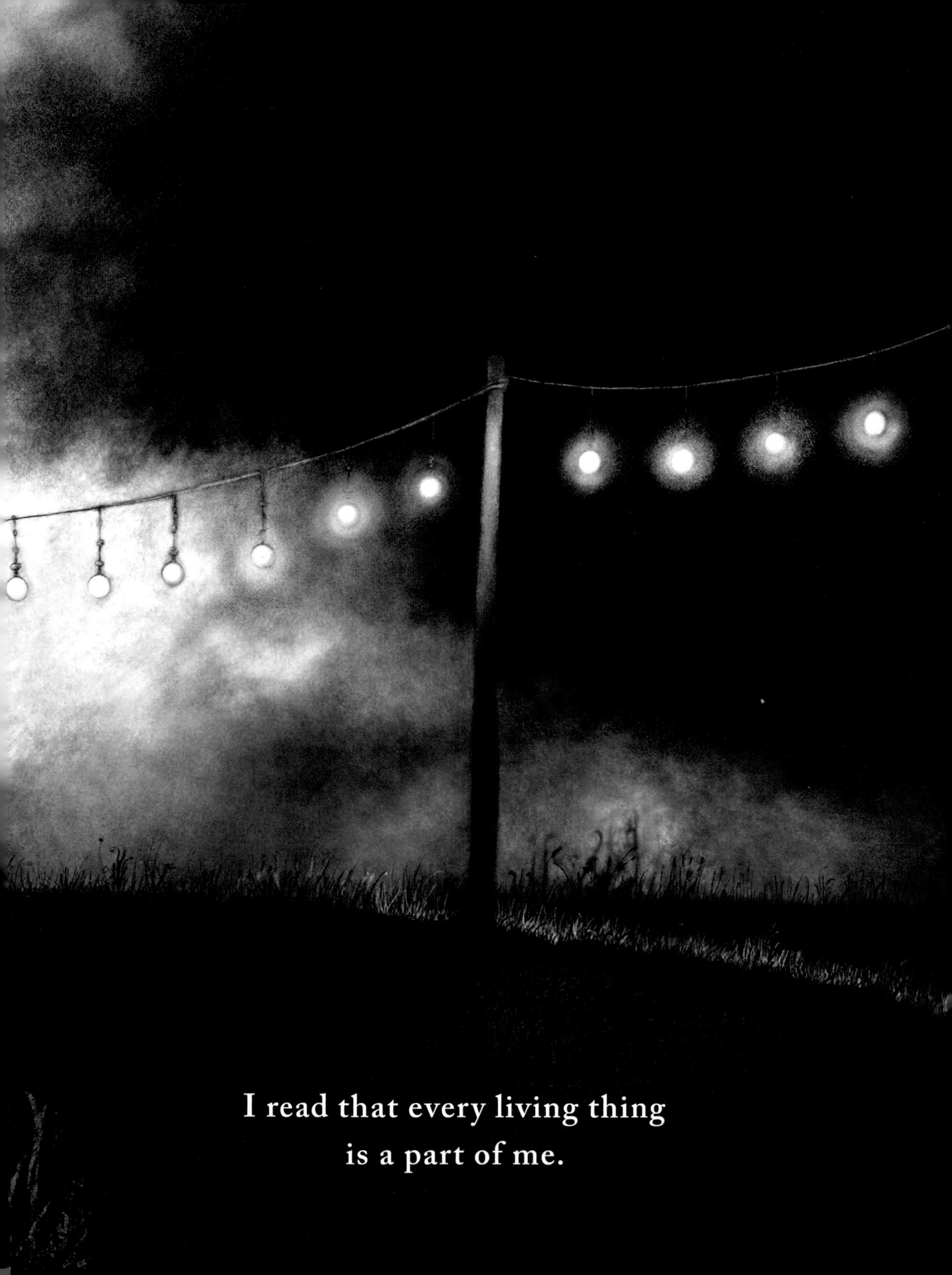

I read that every living thing
is a part of me.

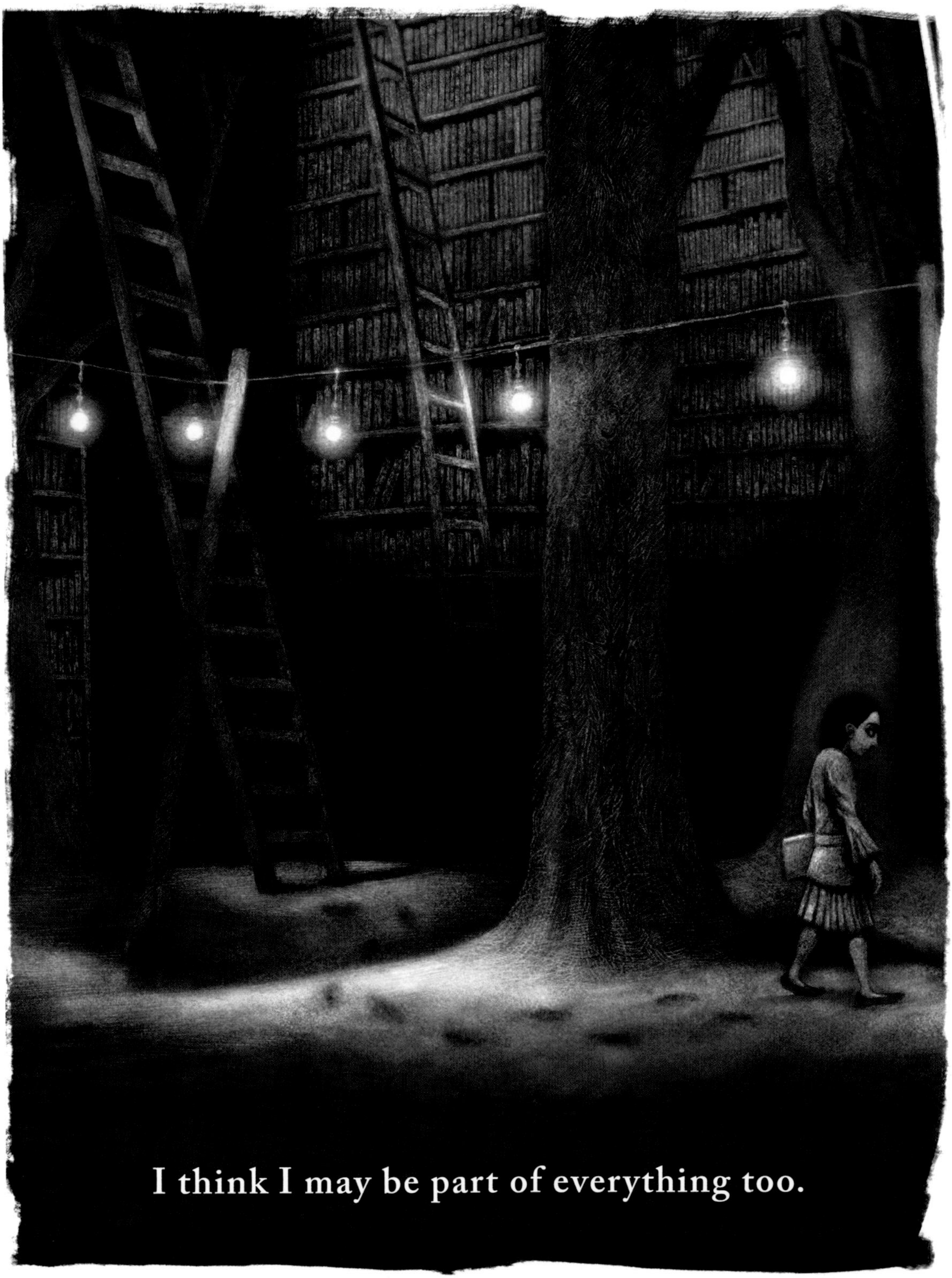

I think I may be part of everything too.

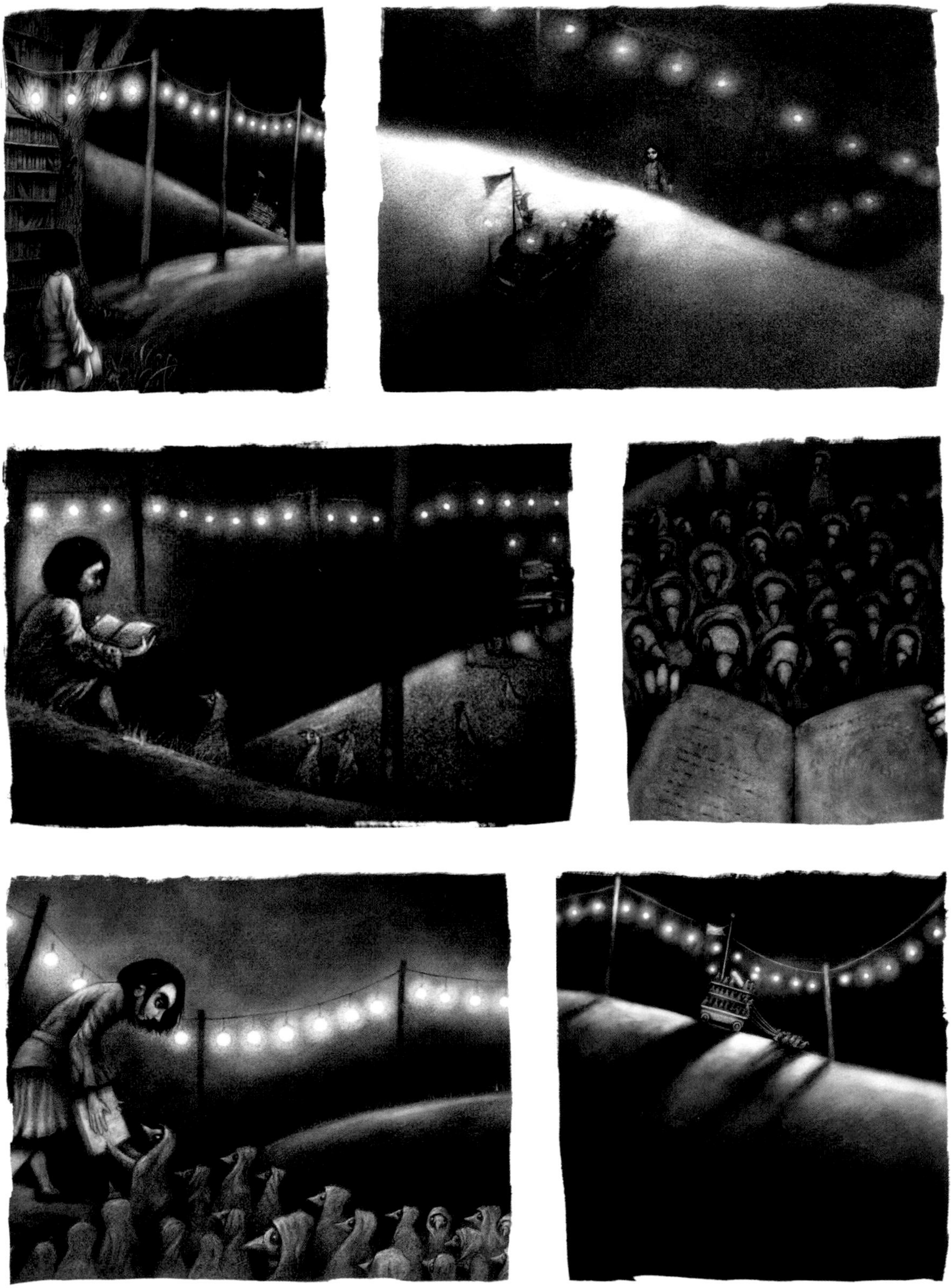

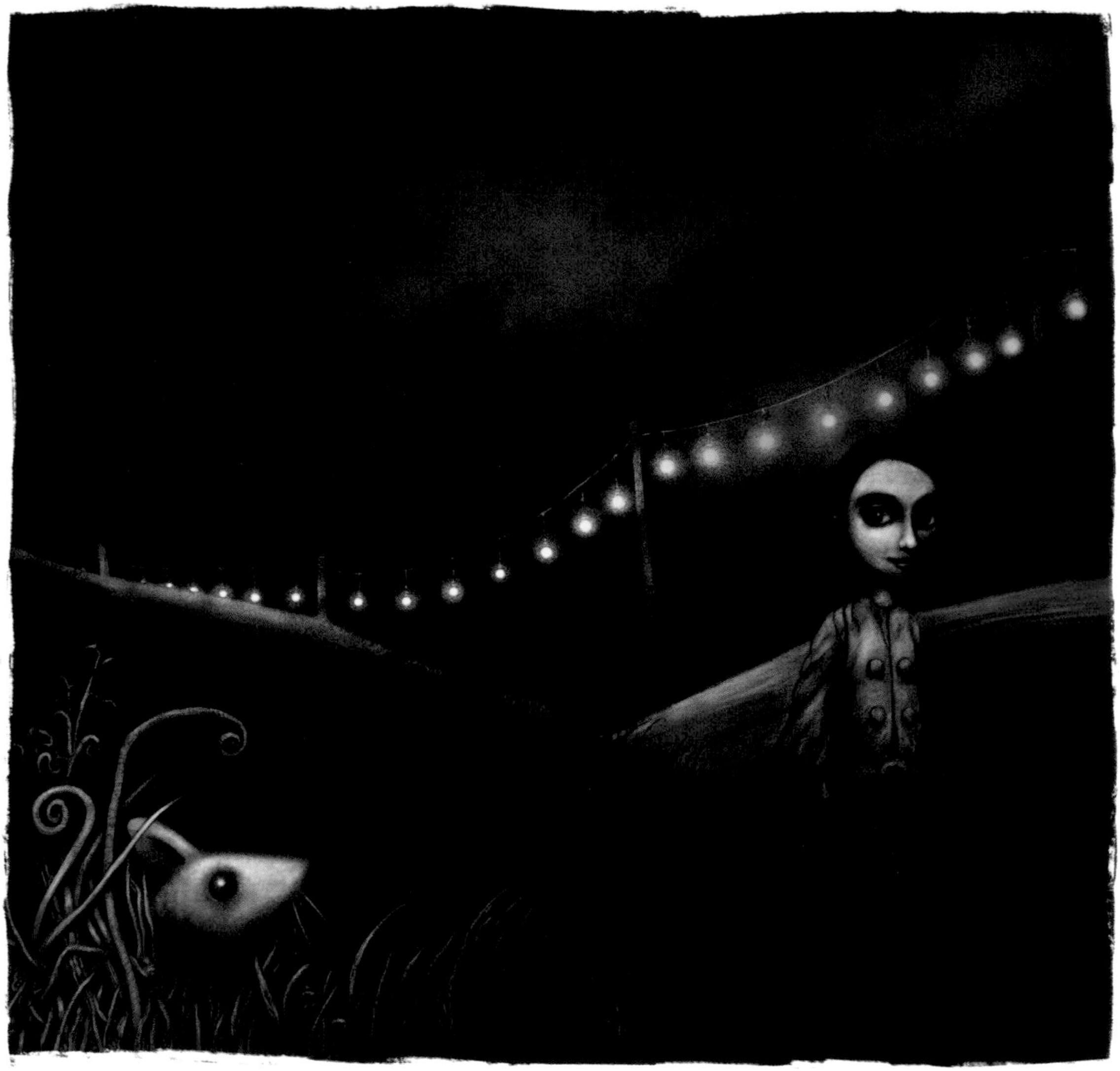

I am not so different.

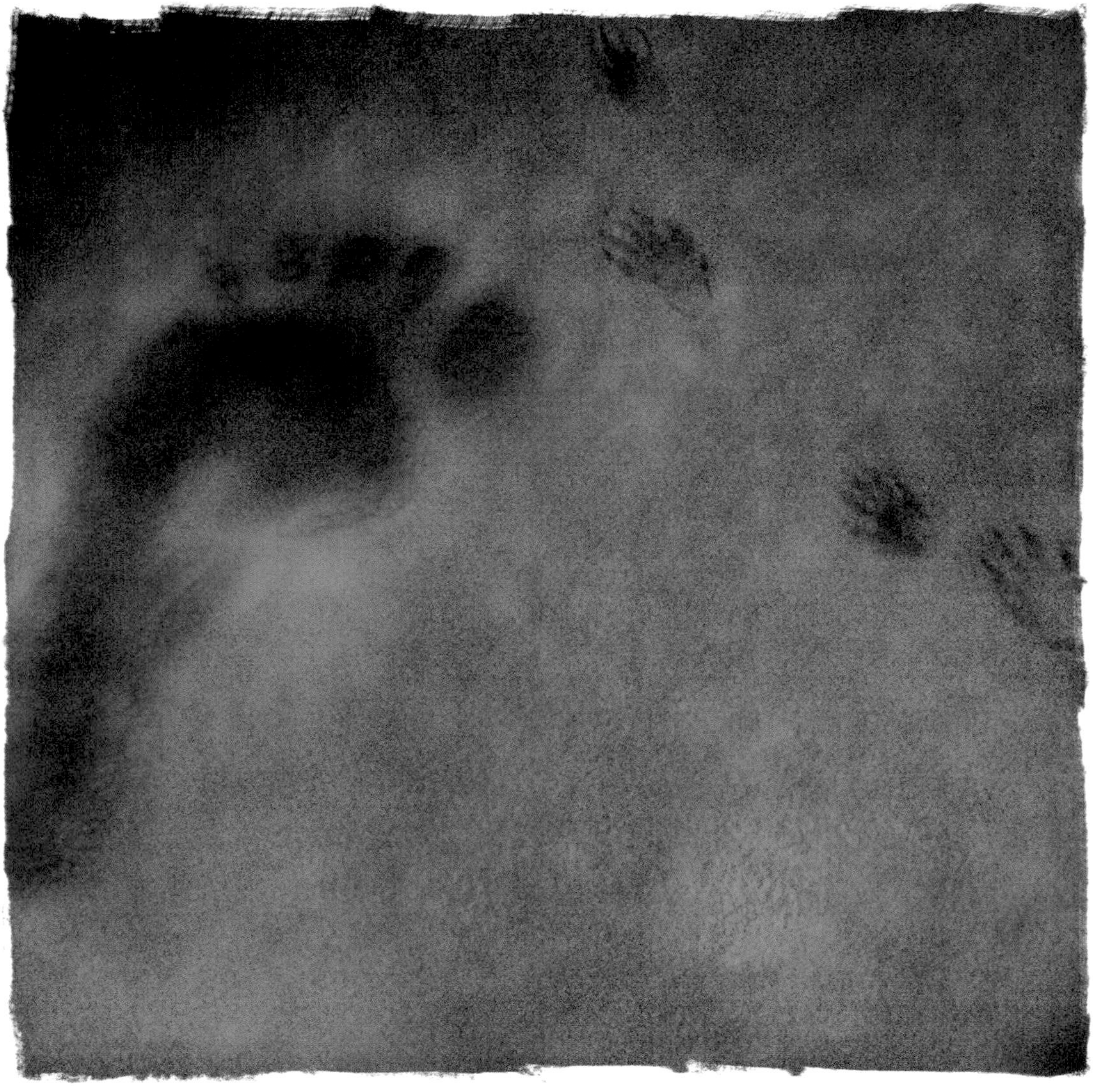

And I am not small.

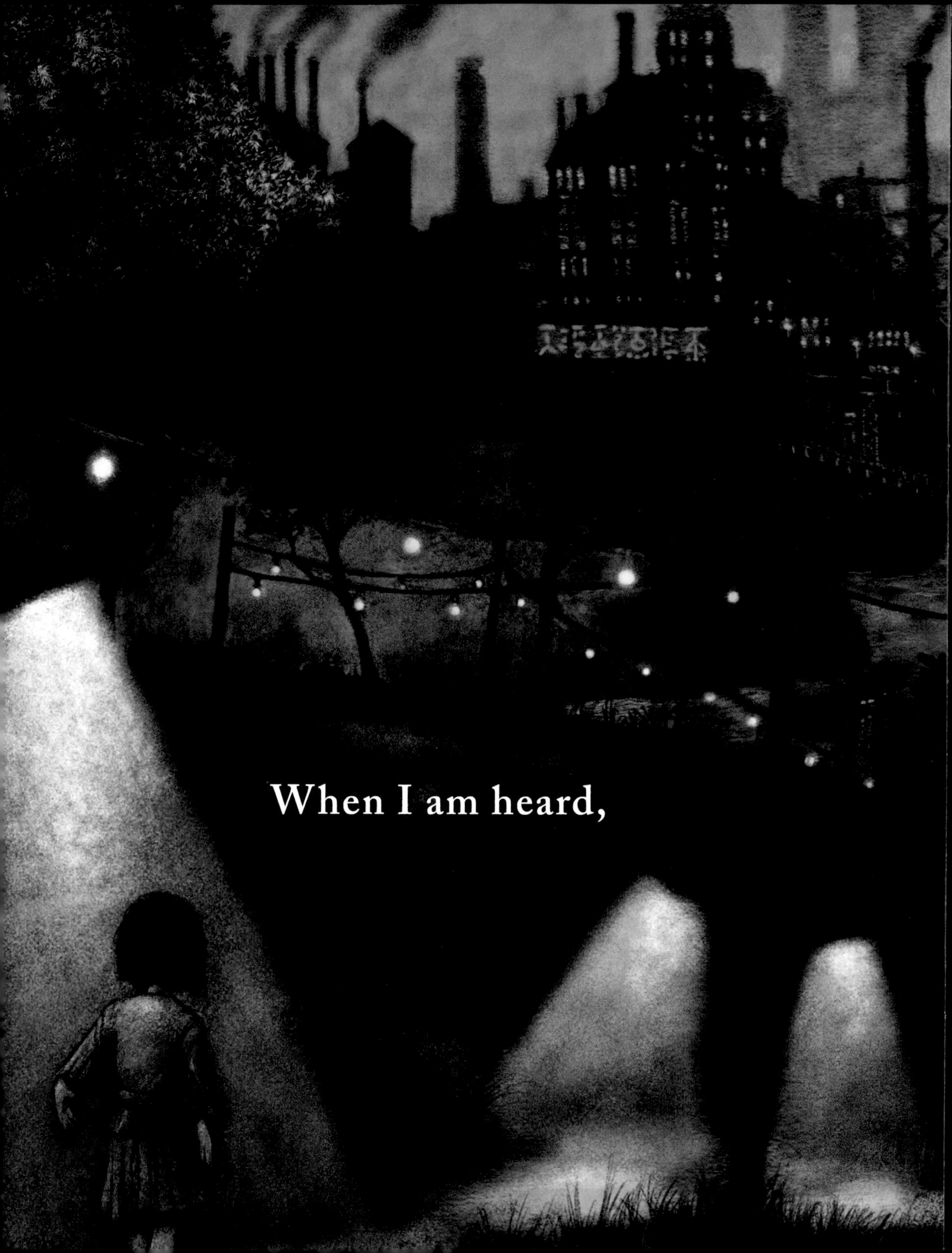

When I am heard,

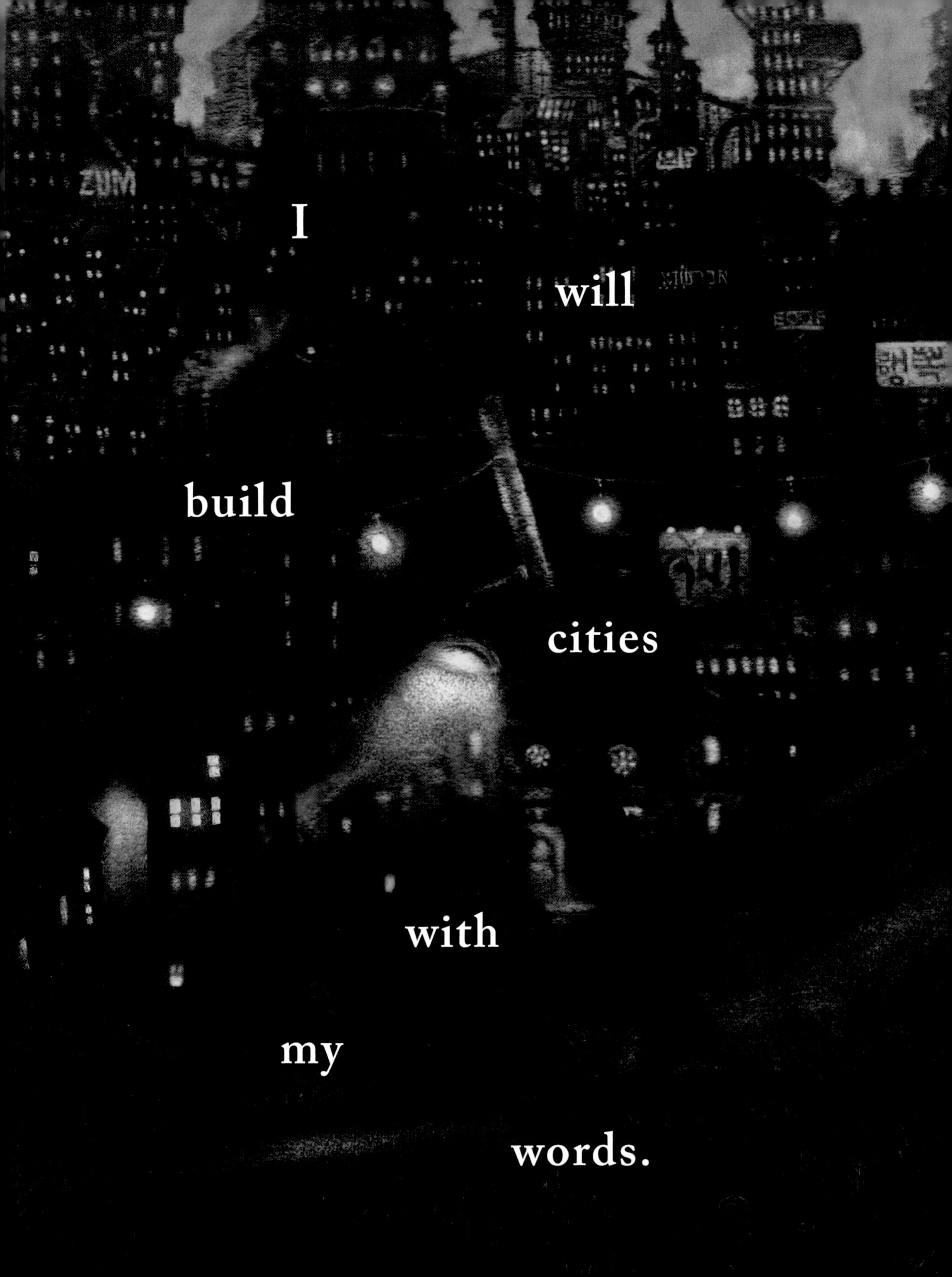

I will build cities with my words.

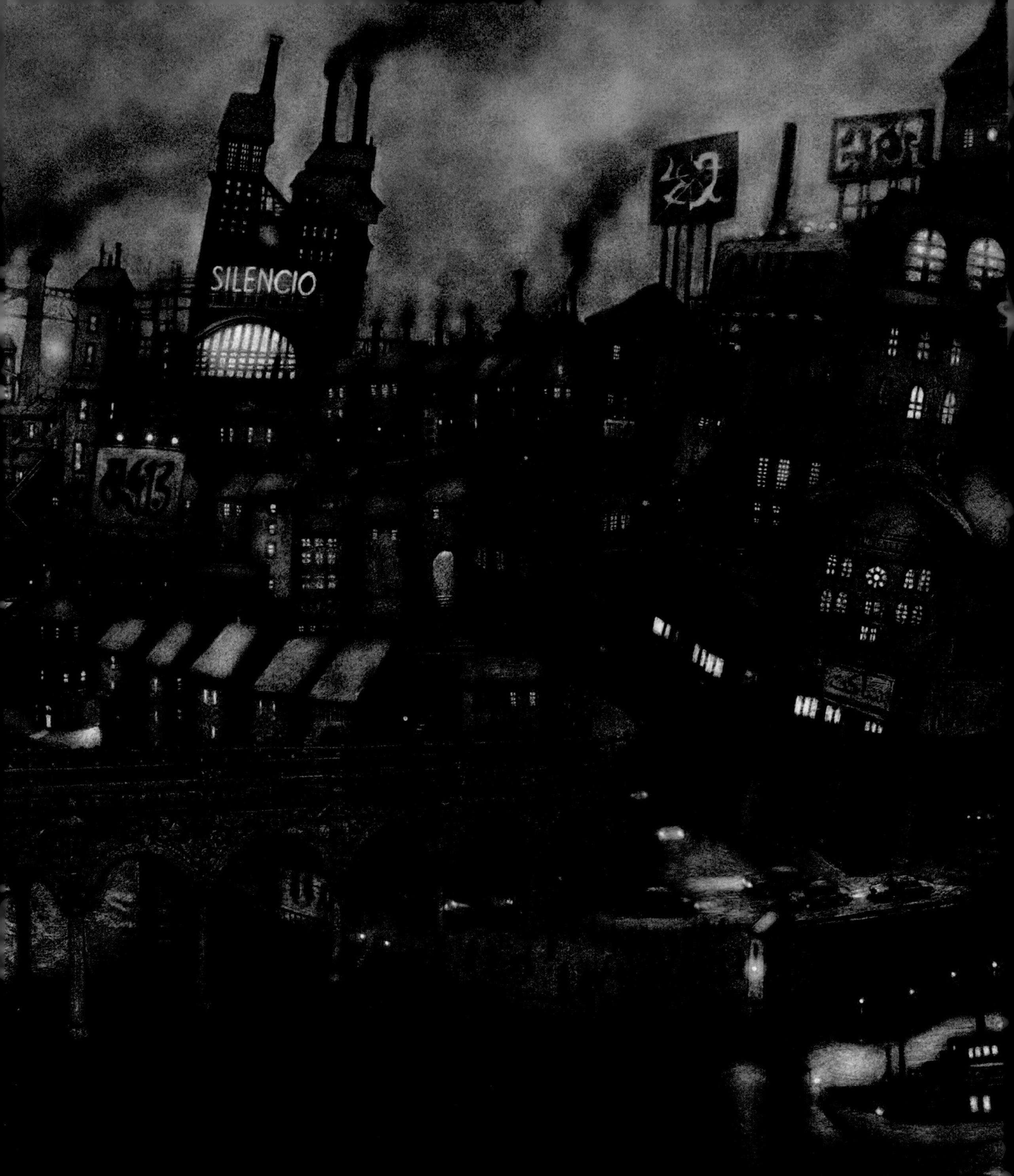
SILENCIO

They will not be quiet

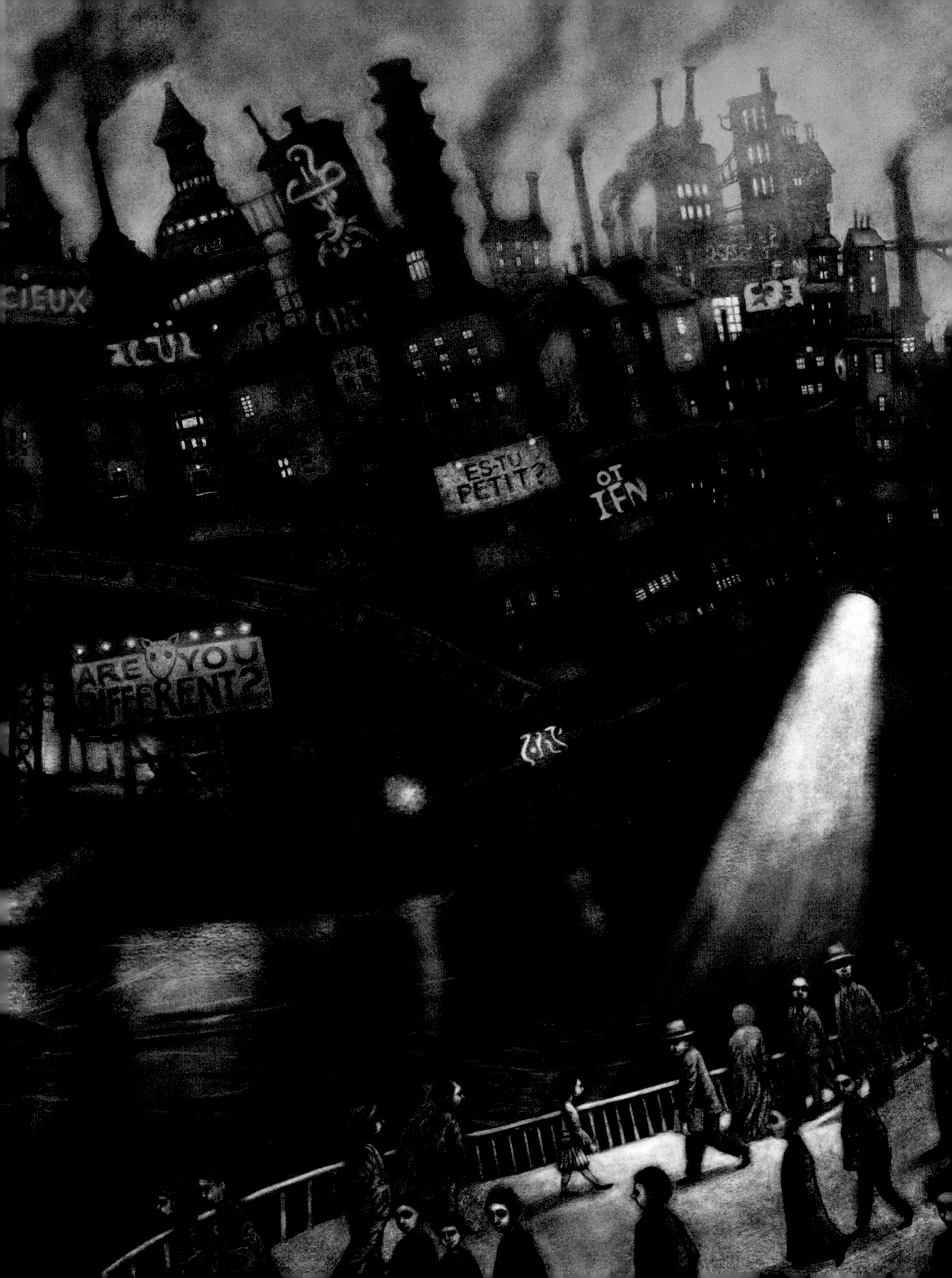
ES-TU PETIT?
ARE YOU DIFFERENT?

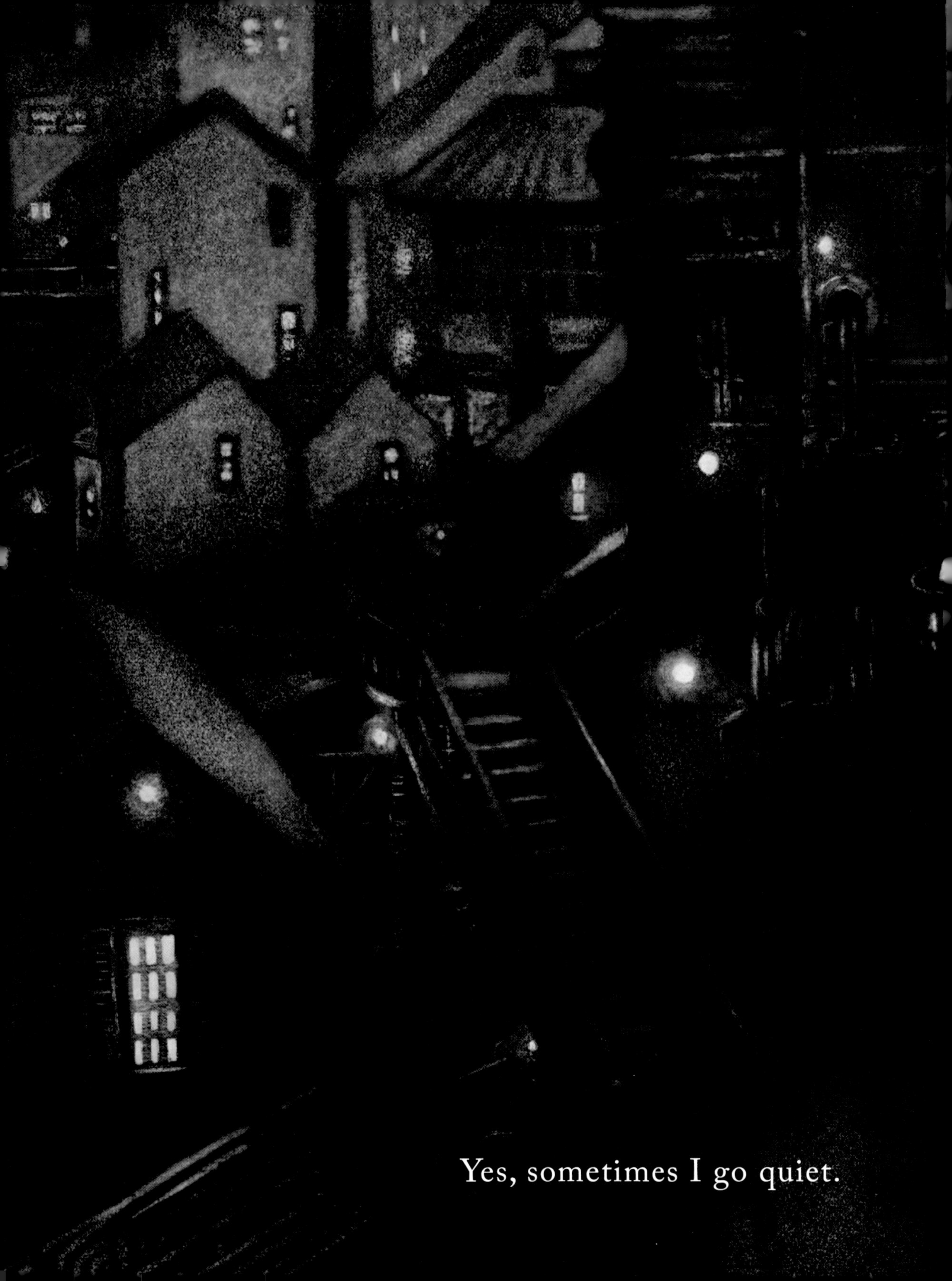

Yes, sometimes I go quiet.

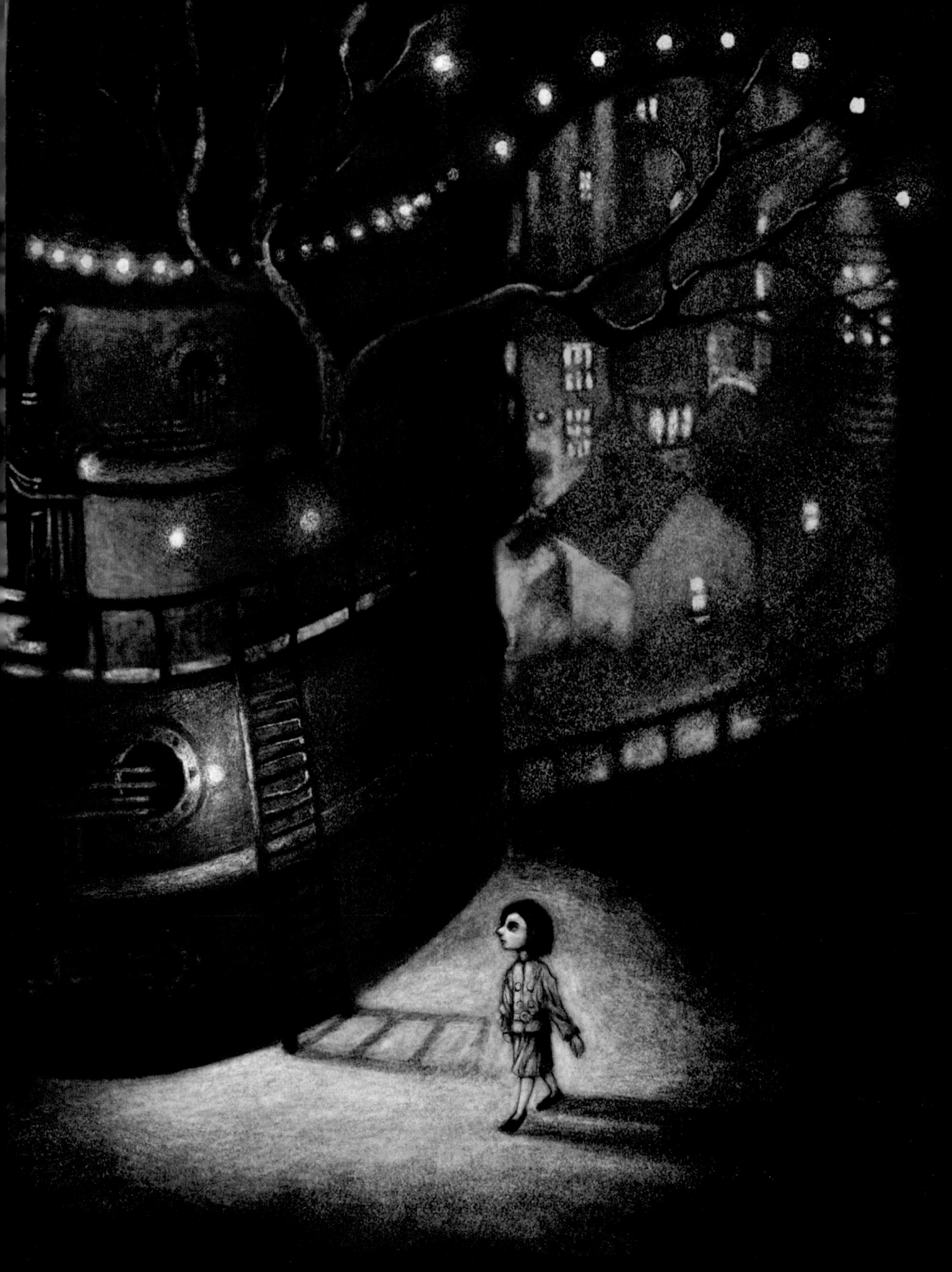

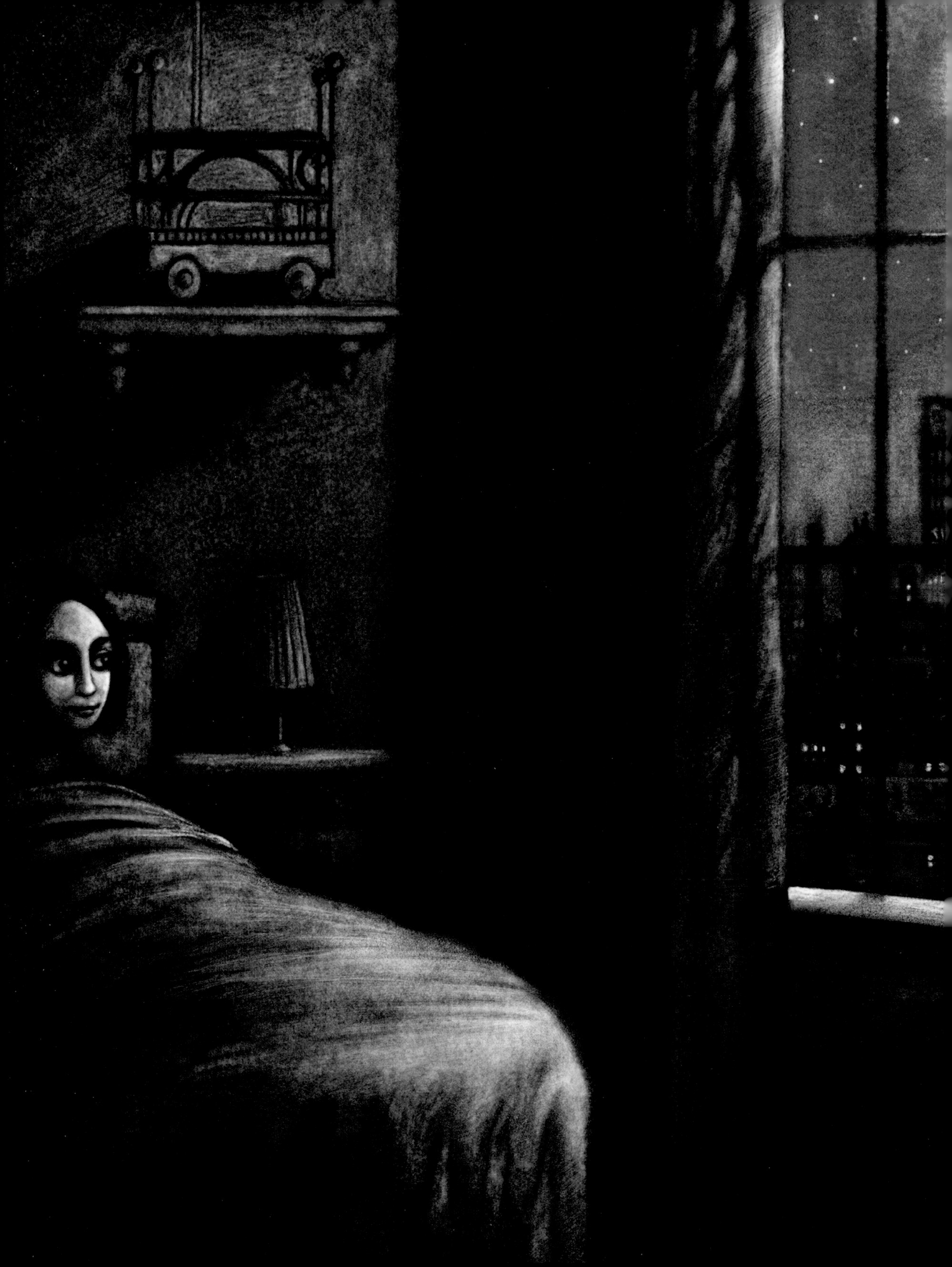

But some day I will make
a shimmering
noise.

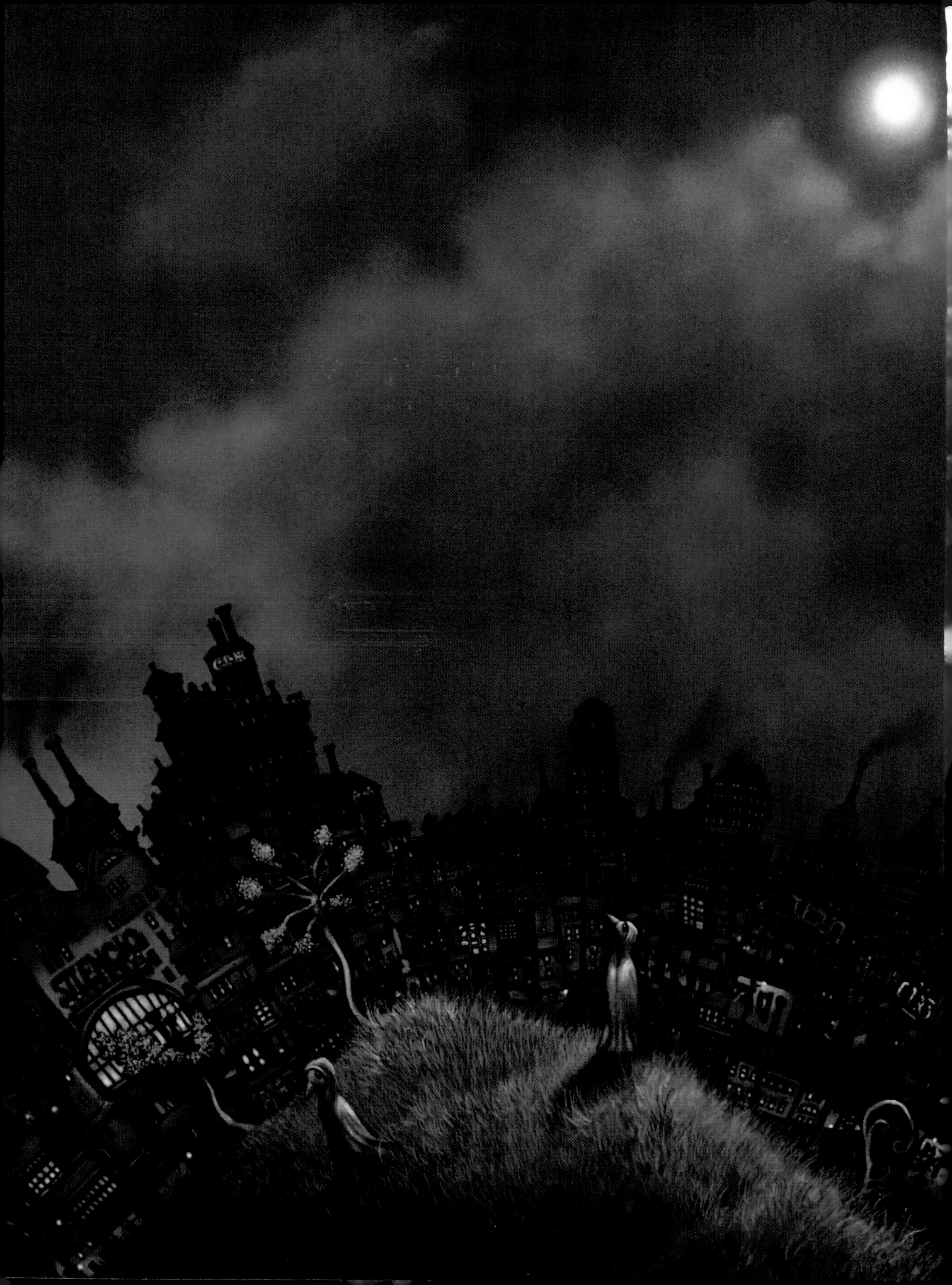